D1551456

WELCOME HOME

SHORT FICTION

S. J. VARENGO

NORTHERN LAKE PUBLISHING

Library of Congress Control Number: 2017908891

For Kimmy, forever.

ALSO BY S. J. VARENGO

The Clean Up Crew Series

The Beauty of Bucharest

The Count of Carolina

The Terror of Tijuana

The Shelby Alexander Thriller Series

Serenity Reborn

The SpyCo Thriller Series

Assignment: Paris

Assignment: Istanbul

Assignment: Sydney

Assignment: Dublin

Assignment: London

The Cerah of Quadar Series

A Dark Clock

Many Hidden Rooms

A Single Candle

Short Fiction

Welcome Home

CONTENTS

A MOMENT OF RELUCTANT FAITH

My mother was dying. The doctors had called us together, sat us down and explained the certainty of it all. They defined the mechanics of it, and offered their best guess at the time frame. Regarding the last, one of the younger oncologists had said something meant, ostensibly, to comfort us, I suppose. He said, "She's probably got a few weeks left, but you never know. Some people are stubborn and don't follow our schedule." I'd thought it hideously funny, but under the circumstances I did not laugh.

I sat with my two sisters, both quietly crying. Once they'd finished reading us the blueprint of our mother's demise, they left us alone in one of those drab, nondescript hospital rooms that were there just so that there was a place to tell you that the one constant in your life would soon be gone.

Theresa, the oldest of us, was the first to speak. "What do we do now?" she asked. Reesa, as I had called her since first attempting to speak her name, was twenty-two. She was quite beautiful and as big sisters go, had always been a pretty good one. Better than twenty-year-old Anne, the "goofy blonde," as we stereotypically dubbed her. She was also very attractive, but being two years older than me, she had made it her mission to bust my balls ever since we'd been little. So constant was her disapproval of my behavior that I was guiltily pleased that the devastating news of mom's impending mortality had given her something else to focus on for five freaking minutes.

"I don't know, Reesa," I said. Then, after a moment, "Should we try to get hold of Dad?" Anne's face immediately morphed into her familiar frown. Of all of us, she was the one who held the hottest grudge, and had since our father had left the family. It had been quite some time ago, (I was seven when the door slammed for the last time), and the truth of the matter was that none of us knew where he was anyway.

"Why waste time searching for *him?*" Anne asked, acid in her voice. "Do you honestly think he gives a shit?"

"I don't know," I said. "I doubt it." That was the end of that conversation.

"I guess that right now we should be focused on Mom," Theresa said. "If they're right and she only has a few weeks, we should probably do our best to make them good ones for her."

We agreed that this was a sound plan, and Anne suggested that we draw up a list of things that would make her remaining time the most enjoyable. Anne was big on lists. They rattled off a few things right away, like keeping her room filled with flowers, and making sure she got her favorite things to eat instead of vile hospital food. To me, though, all of this sounded sickeningly superficial and I thought that if I was the one who was dying none of it would provide me much comfort. But in spite of my reputation for being something of an asshole, I kept my reservations to myself. The act of planning seemed to give the girls comfort.

I suddenly realized that we'd been in the consultation room, surrounded by its sterile green walls, for almost an hour, and suggested that we go visit Mom. When we came in she was watching one of her god-awful soap operas. It had been a week since they'd finished the last round of chemo, and the seven days had been good to her. Sitting up in the bed, she actually looked relatively healthy, and it made me mad that she could look so good and yet be so doomed.

When I picture the scene now, with all the wisdom of the enlightened Twenty-first Century, I am amazed that in 1977 there was an ashtray on her hospital bedside table. Even at the time I'd felt it was odd that they'd let her continue to smoke, especially since she was on oxygen some of the time. But there it was. She'd had us bring it from the house. It was an old-fashioned, ugly thing with a sand-filled, red and black plaid cloth base and a metal insert which was divided into two sides by a row of indentations meant for holding your cigarette while you were doing something slightly less self-destructive. The groove in the middle was big enough to hold a cigar, while the ones at either end were so small it would have been difficult to jam a pin-joint in there. As the only one of us who had ever smoked marijuana, I assumed this detail was probably lost on everyone else. Next to the ashtray was a pack of Benson and Hedges 100's, menthol. It was both Mom's only vice, and her death warrant. When we were young she would sometimes light up and say, "Another nail in the ol' coffin." Not anymore, though. She still smoked, but she didn't joke about it. And when one of the girls tried to get her to stop, she'd shake her head and say, "Don't you think it's a little late to worry about it now?"

The only other thing on the table was a bible, so tattered that it looked like someone had pounded it with a hammer. Mom had read it into that condition. I'd have just as soon beaten it.

My mother's faith was an area in which we had never agreed. She believed in a loving Savior who would one day return in glory and gather His own, marching them triumphantly to Heaven.

I believed in Rock and Roll. I guess that sounds a bit glib, but to this day I still turn to John Lennon and not St. John. I felt that paradise was to be sought in this life, because once the Big Light flickered out the only thing one had to look forward to was gradual decomposition. Over the years we'd stopped arguing about it, having come to a fragile truce.

"My three beans!" Mom said as we walked in. She'd always called us that. Never made a damn bit of sense to me, but it still made me smile. The girls returned her greeting, and I waved. She told us to sit, and I took my place by her feet on the bed, leaving the two very uncomfortable gray plastic and metal chairs for my sisters. They immediately launched into a round of "girl talk," a putrid diversion in my opinion, but again, it made Mom happy. I looked out of her window and wished I was high.

After this had gone on for what seemed to me to be about six days, Mom seemed to remember that I was there. "How's the team doing?" she asked, referring to my high school baseball team.

Still looking out the window I replied, "About as shitty as ever." Mistake. I could feel the daggers plunging into me as my sisters gave me their withering stares. Although their vocabulary was far from puritanical, they never swore in front of Mom, knowing how she felt about it.

I expected a reprimand, but instead she just said, "Oh well.

Keep plugging, Capitán." I didn't really know what to think about that. I had broken one of her cardinal rules, and she had not reacted. Was she finally growing tolerant or had she not been listening? Or did she figure it didn't matter anymore? Whatever the reason, it was the last time she talked to me until we were leaving, and then it was just, "See ya later."

THE CAR RIDE home was extremely unpleasant. The girls took turns laying into me, telling me what an ungrateful prick I was for upsetting Mom, "especially now." I made the weak argument that it hadn't seemed to upset her, but they brushed that aside and launched into a fresh assault. So, I sat silently until we got home, at which point I bolted out of the car, unlocked the house and ran upstairs to my room. Once inside I locked and toweled the door, then smoked myself into a calmer shade of life. "Sgt. Pepper" was working its magic on me at thirty-three and a third rounds per minute. Insulated from my sisters' rage and away from that god-awful hospital, I started to feel a little less horrible.

Eventually I fell asleep, lights still on and fully clothed. I had a dream about Mom. It was something that had really happened: a trip to Disney World when I was five. It was all happiness and sunshine at first. Dad was there as well, but was always a few yards behind us. While Mom and we three kids were giddy as could be, he did not smile. Even at that tender age I could tell that Mom was working extra hard to make sure that we had the time of our lives, in an effort to make up for Dad's obvious sour attitude. She made sure we experienced everything the Magic Kingdom had to offer, right down to the mouse-ear hats with our names written on them in glitter. Mine said "Scootch," which had been my nickname from infancy. The dream ended just before the tremendous argument Mom and Dad had while we were in line for the Haunted Mansion. So when I woke up I was feeling happy, remembering all the things Mom had done for us that day. But the dream had been so vivid that as I laid in bed and thought about it, I soon recalled the fight. Then I remembered how Dad had hit me shortly after because I tried to hold his hand.

The house was silent, save for the ticking of Mom's beloved grandfather clock, which stood in the hallway outside of our bedroom doors. After a few minutes I fell back to sleep, lulled by its ancient rhythm.

WHEN I WOKE UP AGAIN, it was to full-fledged, screaming sunlight. I turned to look at my alarm clock, and saw that I had beaten it to the draw by a few minutes. I reached over and shut it off before it could do anything drastic.

I began the process of getting ready for school. First, I smoked a joint. Then I showered, shaved, and ran downstairs to consume two quick bowls of Cap'n Crunch and a high protein milkshake. I was, after all, a star athlete. I heard the bus coming down the street just as I was wiping the chocolaty foam from my mouth.

The school day was uneventful until I told my girlfriend Donna what the doctors had said. Her sobbing was so loud that I eventually had to take her outside, where I held her until she regained her composure. The whole thing was tremendously embarrassing, but I was inwardly grateful that she had shed the tears I could not.

Do not think that I was cold and unaffected by the news of my mother's eminent departure. I had always pictured her as some kind of unbeatable trooper. She'd survived years of verbal abuse, beating and finally abandonment at the hands of my father. She'd maintained a quiet love for me, even after I had donned the mantle of black sheep. I had loved her all my life. Even when I was screaming at her during my most rebellious stage I knew that I loved her. I was just a teenager. And a dick. To lose her meant losing the last thread that was holding our family together.

But I could not cry for her. I had not cried since the day our father had peeled out of the driveway, eleven years before. I had suffered broken bones and broken hearts, but had never once shed a tear. I had forgotten how. So Donna's breakdown that day was intensely cathartic.

I went through baseball practice robotically, and when it was done I changed out of my sweaty workout clothes and walked to the bus stop two blocks from school, where I caught the 5:15 downtown. The hospital rose ominously in the distance as I hiked toward it. The image of Norman Bates's weathered old house in *Psycho* came to mind.

By the time I got to Mom's room the girls had come and gone. I could tell they'd been there because the room was literally polluted with wildflowers, and I detected the smell of Reesa's spaghetti sauce lingering in the room. Obviously they had begun their campaign to make Mom's final days as pleasant as possible. She was gazing dreamily at the ceiling, half-smiling, when I walked in. "Hi guy," she said.

"Hello, Queen-mother," I replied. "How goes it?"

Still smiling, she said, "It's starting to hurt pretty bad again." This admission caught me off guard. The last time she'd been really bad, before her previous round of chemo and radiation, when every cough had been so painful that she was constantly

7

fighting back tears, she'd never said a word about it. She'd just collect herself after her fit and go on as if nothing had happened.

"I'm sorry," I said, immediately realizing how inane that sounded. She just nodded her head and I felt a chill.

"Listen to me, Scootch," she said. I looked her in the eyes, vaguely aware that it was the first time I'd done so in quite a while. "I have some things I need to say to you now. You know that pretty soon you and the girls are going to be all alone in this world, save for each other."

"Mom, don't," I said weakly, finding myself increasing unsettled by her frankness.

"Don't interrupt," she whispered. I shut up. "I know we've always called you 'the baby,' and we've always pretty much treated you that way. But I've got a secret for you. In a lot of ways, you grew up a lot faster than your sisters. For all Reesa and Anne's adult bluster, they're still basically silly little girls. You've technically been the man of the house for a long time now. You haven't always been the most responsible man I've ever known, but you've always been one tough cookie.

"Well the time is coming for that strength to mature. When I go those big girls are going to turn into helpless, lost babies. And just at the time when someone needs to be thinking straight. I'm afraid that's going to be your job. There are a lot of strings attached to dying. You'd think it would be easy. You just stop living, right? But no, there's funeral plans, burial plots, the will... I've actually taken care of most of that stuff already, but there are still going to be several business matters left to deal with. That will be your responsibility, understand?"

I felt ill. It was difficult to follow along with what she was saying. My brain wanted to shut down. But I must have managed to nod, because she smiled and said, "Good. I knew I could count on you."

She was quiet for several minutes, just gazing into my eyes. I had forgotten how pretty she was, both because I had rarely looked at her during the past few difficult years and because cancer is not known for its beautifying effects. But as I peered deeply into her dark brown eyes she suddenly became the personification of loveliness.

"One more thing, my brave young man. I know you don't share my faith in God. It's been something like five years since the last time you let me drag you to church. But I want you to know this absolutely: whenever you feel lonely, whenever you miss me, know that I am always watching over you from a far better, far more wonderful place. And, no matter what you do, I will always love you."

I WALKED ALL the way home from the hospital in a state of shock. It was nearly four in the morning when I finally came in. Reesa was in the kitchen, heating up some milk on the stove. Her housecoat was dimly illuminated by the light over the range. "Couldn't sleep," she said. "Want some cocoa? Might sober you up." I usually reacted pretty angrily to her off-hand accusations, even when she was right. But tonight it rolled right off. I don't think anything she could have said would have been able to make me feel any worse than I already did.

"Not drunk," I said. "But sure, I'll have a cup with you." I could see her expression in the stove light. It was surprise. She'd laid the bait for an argument, but I hadn't taken it.

"Hey, are you okay?" she asked, switching on the ceiling light. She put her hand on my shoulder.

"Yeah...no... Oh, Reesa, I don't know. I went to see Mom after baseball and I guess the reality of this all kind of hit me tonight." The milk was hot, and I made the two cups of chocolate. I handed over hers with a visibly shaky hand. We went into the living room and switched on the TV. Anne must have heard us, because after a few minutes she came downstairs.

"What's going on?" she asked, brushing the blonde hair out of her sleepy eyes. I pointed to the stove and held up my cup; vague sign language intended to tell her to make herself a mug and join us. She used the last of the hot milk, then sat next to me on the sofa. "Are you in trouble or something?" she asked me, only a hint of reproach in her voice. I had to laugh.

"No, Annie-Fannie," I said, using her tease-name. "I'm fine. Just a little shook up. Mom and I had a long talk tonight about...preparations. It made me realize that she's *really* going to die. I – I don't want her to, Annie. I don't think I can handle it." Before I knew what was happening, I began to cry. I didn't actually realize what was happening at first, thinking my eyes were blurry because I was so tired. But when the first tear broke loose and hit my cheek, I exploded into convulsive sobbing. Anne threw her arms around me and Reesa ran over, kneeling on the floor in front of me and putting her hands on my quaking knees. They were soon crying as well. And even though I knew I was supposed to be strong, the "tough cookie," as Mom had said, I couldn't stop. We were all about to lose the greatest treasure in our lives and we could do nothing about it, aside from express the black grief that was strangling us all.

After a very long time we found ourselves all cried-out. I got up and walked to the big picture window. The sun was coming up. I pointed to it, and the girls got up and stood beside me. We put our arms around each other and watched the sky grow brighter. Then there was a second dawning: I realized that I had to get ready for school. I went to my room and pulled myself together. It wasn't until much later in the day that I realized that for the first time in a couple of years I'd gone to school without getting high first. And despite my breakdown that early morning, I felt oddly strengthened.

TWO WEEKS LATER, it was obvious the end was very near. Mom's condition had deteriorated so rapidly that every time I went to see her I could literally see her dying right before my eyes.

We had begun taking turns spending the night with her, and on one of my nights, as I dozed in the chair beside her bed, I dreamt that the doctor was telling me that she was gone. It was the first time this had entered into my dreaming mind. I woke with a start. Mom's breathing was labored and ragged. It was three in the morning. I left the room and found a payphone. My fingers were trembling as I called the house. Reesa answered.

"Rees, I think this is it. You'd better wake Annie and get down here as quick as you can."

When I went back into her room, Mom was awake, but she wasn't aware of my presence. She was fully engaged in a conversation. I just stood there and listened, and after a moment I realized that she thought she was talking to Jesus. The one-sided exchange went on for about twenty minutes, Mom talking in her raspy voice. I could tell that the very act of speaking was causing her agony, but she didn't stop until the girls entered the room, and she said, "What, Lord? They're all here now? Oh, good!"

With great effort she turned her head to face us. I could see her eyes struggling to focus. The girls began crying, but I, at least for the moment, seemed to have forgotten how once more. For several minutes she just looked at us, shifting her eyes from one to another, smiling through her unimaginable pain. Finally, in a tattered voice that was no more than a whisper she said, "Pray with me."

I stiffened a little, not having anticipated this. My over-taxed mind jumped to Joyce's description of Stephen Dedalus's refusal to pray with his mother when it was her dying wish. There was no God my life, especially at this dreadful instant. But I could not torture her in her final moments as Dedalus had done. I looked to my sisters. They stood with their hands clasped and their eyes closed, but they could not speak. Mom turned her clouded gaze to me. I bowed my head, terrified.

"I won't dishonor my mother by lying. I do not believe in you. But I am a fool in more ways than one. I've been wrong many times. And my mother *does* believe. She always has, even in times that I felt proved you were a lie. If anyone deserves to be with you, it is this woman. So, if you are there, I'm begging you to love her as we do...as I do."

I couldn't think of anything more to say. When I opened my eyes, my mother's face seemed to me to be glowing, giving off a blinding radiance. My sisters were still standing there, but it felt to me like Mom and I were alone. Her smile beamed at me, and with the last bit of strength that she had, she lifted her weary hand and caressed my cheek. I reached up and took her hand in mine, and held it until a moment later when she gave me a final squeeze, then went limp. I laid her arm across her chest, and went to get the doctor.

WELCOME HOME

You're getting closer
To pushing me off of life's little edge
'Cause I'm a loser
And sooner or later you know I'll be dead
- 3 Doors Down

Most mornings Sid's first thought was, "My head *really* hurts."

Today, introspective for some reason, he thought, "How many days in a row has my head hurt when I woke up?" How many indeed. How deep the ocean? How high the stars? Who fucking cares? He didn't move for a few minutes. Moving made it worse. Eventually he knew that he'd have to lift his pounding head, if only to figure out where he was. But perhaps he could gather some clues without going there just yet.

Alright. It was dark, but his unfailing internal chronometer told him it must be daytime. He brought his wristwatch up close to his eyes and fumbled with the buttons on the side. After a few attempts he got the back light to fire up and the LED digits confirmed that it was indeed 8:00 a.m.

"So it's dark, but it's morning." He assumed that the death of the sun would have made it colder; his sweat-soaked shirt ruled that out. So he was probably in a room with no windows. Sid had a lot of friends who let him squat, but only two that had window-less rooms. Carol, a waitress co-worker who he called "Bird," had a bathroom situated in the geographical center of her apartment. They joked that it would be to this room that they ran when the next tornado came through Potsdam. As far as either of them knew, there had never been a tornado in northern New York. They'd used the room for many other wonderful things, but never as a storm shelter. Still, why be unprepared?

But Bird had not talked to him since she'd seen him kissing her best friend. That had happened two weeks ago, allegedly. Sid had absolutely no memory of the event, but then again there was a reason his head hurt every morning. It was because he drank every night until *nothing* hurt. So there were many things that he tended not to remember, and there were many things he did that he shouldn't have done. This most serious faux pas was one of them. As he lay in the dark thinking about it, he doubted, given the high tally of shots he'd started drinking at nine the night before that he'd done anything to earn his was back into her good graces. This wasn't Bird's bathroom.

Which meant he was probably in Ron's basement flat. It felt as though he was laying on a futon; further evidence. There was a futon crammed in the back corner of the extra bedroom, which Ron used mainly to store boxes of things he did not use but did not wish to part with. Sid often ended up there, for he had not managed to ruin his friendship with Ron, thus far. *I'm just another thing that's unused but not quite ready for the trash*, he thought. He and Ron shared a bond which had formed instantly the day they met and had proven unshakeable. They just didn't let anything the other guy did bother them. It was a rare and vital connection.

Still not ready to move the ticking bomb attached to his neck, but satisfied that he now knew where he was, Sid considered the ebb and flow of friends and acquaintances in his life. Though hugely unsuccessful at life in general, he did have an aptitude for finding good friends. Despite having earned his bachelor's degree two years prior, Sid now worked at Maxwell's Restaurant and was firmly ensconced in the food service subculture. Sid found that working in a restaurant was like being in a large family. There was a definite pecking order. Lane, the owner, sat Zeus-like atop his Olympus, Sid and the other dishwashers were firmly planted at the bottom, unquestionably in Hades. In between came everyone else, maintenance, wait staff, hostesses, cashiers and, just a rung down from the peak, the bartenders. Everybody lived with everybody, they partied together, and they were there for you when things got bad.

But as with any family there was dysfunction. The copious amounts drugs and alcohol consumed by literally every Maxwell's employee virtually ensured that. It was like being a rock star without having to tune your guitar. And when you dealt with individuals whose personalities were more than a little shaped by the chemicals they consumed it meant that some friends came and others went, but that no one ever came too close or went very far.

Things were especially fluid when it came to women. Though only twenty-five, Sid was divorced. He'd married Melinda, who he'd met in high school while dating her friend. After eight intense months that relationship came to an end when the girl-friend started seeing another guy, who she eventually married. Melinda had shown him kindness during his inevitable period of heartbreak, which he mistook for enduring love. She'd apparently been fooled as well, for a season. They migrated to the North Country, went to college together and got married at the end of her freshman year. But within three years of till death do us part, she parted and Sid started working on the death.

Since then there had been a series of women who had shown him kindness, but he no longer allowed himself to read anything into the act. Not that he wasn't a giving, caring lover. When he was with a woman he tried to treat her as though she was the only other person in the world. But every one of them came to realize that he had a first love, and her name was Self Destruction.

Because for Sid there was no point. Not to education. College had just been something he'd done for four years to delay starting his life in earnest. Likewise, there was no point in career. He washed dishes for a living! Scraping someone's half-eaten strip steak and Brussel sprouts into the gray Rubbermaid garbage can before standing the plate on edge in its metal rack, slamming down the door and pushing the red switch to the right...not something likely to pad your resume or land you in Who's Who. And there was certainly no point in finding someone with whom to share your life. He'd failed twice at that by the time he'd been twenty-three, and now he entered every relationship knowing that sooner or later the booze and drugs with which he was working so hard to kill himself would drive her away, even if they met while drinking gin and snorting lines. Everyone that Sid knew partied to have fun. He did it in a

Herculean effort to stop his heart from beating. Or at least from feeling.

The room suddenly filled with light, and Sid's head exploded. Ron had opened the door, and the recessed bulb in the hallway signaled that the time for self-analysis had ended. "Don't you have to go wash the quiche pans?" Ron asked. Sid focused on his figure, outlined in the piercing light. He was naked. Which meant that somewhere else in the apartment was a woman who was also naked.

"Quiche. Yeah." Sid sat up on the futon and looked around for his pants. After a moment, he realized that he had never taken them off, so he tried to find his sneakers instead. He was still wearing them as well. Finally, he felt around for his glasses. Those he found on the floor. Sensing that he could put it off no longer, he stood up. He pushed past Ron and stumbled to the bathroom, where he immediately threw up, knowing as he did that it wouldn't be the last time he did so before he metabolized the poison and started to feel vaguely human. That usually happened around 4 p.m. Just in time to finish the lunch shift and make it upstairs to the bar for Happy Hour.

After a hardy round of stomach eruption, he undressed and crawled into the narrow white shower. The water felt like hailstones hitting his head.

By the time he came out of the bathroom, Ron had wandered back down the hall. In the living room, wrapped in a fuzzy white blanket, was Bird. Clearly naked beneath the Yeti hide, she didn't make eye contact. Ron was standing above her, ready to pick up where he'd left off when he went to keep Sid from being late for work. His anticipation of the act was unmistakably evident. Her presence did not upset Sid. He'd hurt Bird by kissing her friend, but he felt no reciprocal sense of injustice. He felt nothing. It was

17

what it was. Once she'd been with him, now she was with Ron. And so it goes.

"Alright, man. I'll catch you later," Sid said as he opened the door and stepped out. Looking back over his shoulder he saw that Bird had already shed the blanket. "Enjoy the rest of your morning," he said, closing the door behind him.

Maxwell's was a three-minute walk from Ron's apartment. Five if you stopped to vomit. Which Sid did. Twice. But, being a considerate citizen, he did it in an alley that ran behind some shops and led to the restaurant. It was abandoned at this early hour, so there was no one to be put off by his body's ongoing effort to purge the toxin from his system.

By the time he stumbled through the back door into the kitchen, he was sweating once again, and there was a ringing in his ears. In order to make it to the restroom he would have to climb the stairs that led from the kitchen to the dining room, make his way through the maze of tables and then go down another flight of stairs. That wasn't happening. So he wretched into the trashcan, which it was his duty to empty, eliminating the need to feel guilty. Besides, there wasn't really anything left in his stomach to come back up. Dry heaving was so much worse, though.

Danny, who opened the kitchen at seven every morning and baked the quiche that the trendy lunch patrons so desired, tossed four pie pans into the stainless-steel sink. It sounded like a cherry-bomb. "Jesus, Dan! Do you have to do that every morning?"

"Do you have to start every day by ralphing in my kitchen?" Sid looked at him. Dan, ever the wise-ass, was smiling.

"Yes," Sid said. "Yes I do."

"You need to carry the meat slicer upstairs. Today's the buffet for Tom."

Sid moaned. The slicer was heavy, and the stairs would seem extra steep this morning. And being reminded of the buffet forced him to think about Tom. Although he didn't work at the restaurant, Tom Sebastian was still part of the family. He drank at the bar often, and had entertained the crowd many nights playing his guitar and singing in his plaintive tenor. He was a musician, a genuinely kind human being, and the first person that Sid knew who had succumbed to AIDS.

Sid's employer, Lane, though a hopeless coke-head and a shitty boss in general, never missed a chance to appear philanthropic. Tom had racked up a lot of hospital bills toward the end, and his partner Will had been saddled with them. So, Lane put together a special buffet, the proceeds from which would go to Will, in honor of Tommy. Lane had done the same thing two years before when Gary the janitor had decided to canoe from his house to the liquor store in the wee hours of New Year's Day. They didn't find him till April, when his bloated remains had been fished out of the intake pipe of the water treatment plant. Gary's family was notoriously poor, so Lane picked up the check for his funeral.

All these people just trying to live, Sid thought. *And they're dropping like flies. I'm trying like hell to die, and I wake up every damn morning.* The irony and futility overpowered him. He set the meat slicer on a table, then tripped past the potted ferns and wicker chairs and stumbled down the stairs to the men's room. Dry heaves again, lasting a solid five minutes.

When at last he finished turning his guts inside out, he put his back against the heavily graffiti-marked wall and slowly slid to the floor. He sat there a long time. Long enough for his mind to involuntarily recall that only seven years earlier he'd been an all-state football player, president of the National Honor Society, and had stolen the show in the school's production of *Bye Bye Birdie*, gold lamé suit and all. Now he was sitting in last night's dried piss, cursing his body not for the agony he was experiencing, but because his system kept failing to fail.

A few minutes later, Dan kicked open the door. "What? Did you finally die?" he asked. Sid looked up and shook his head.

"Still no."

"Well then get the fuck back to work. We're gonna be losing our minds in an hour. People always pack these buffets out."

"Let's have a quick beer," Sid said.

Dan looked at him, and Sid tried hard to read the expression on his face. He couldn't. Dan liked his drink, but unlike Sid, it wasn't his religion. "How about a coffee?"

"Don't be obscene," Sid said.

"Alright. Just one," Dan said finally. He walked behind Sid up the stairs, ready to put his hands up should he topple over backwards.

Dan went behind the bar and threw open the sliding metal hatch of one of the coolers, pulling out two cold Canadian beers. The sound of the bottle cap coming off was the first sweet thing Sid had heard all day. They sat beside one another at the bar, not concerned about being discovered having two on the house this early in the morning. They would be the only crew there until almost nine-thirty, when the wait staff arrived and started setting up the dining room.

"You were in rare form last night," Dan said, after taking a long pull.

"Did I kill anybody?" Sid asked. He was only partly kidding. It was always a possibility.

"No. But you did tip over a table. Then you punched some big blonde dude wearing a pink Polo with his collar popped, because you said he'd put the table in your path on purpose."

"Did he kill me?"

"Obviously not, douche. But he wanted to. It took three of us to get him away from you and out the door."

"Home is where you can punch a guy and get him tossed for it."

"I think the pink Polo had a lot to do with it too. A pink Polo, for Christ-sake!"

"Probably a St. Lawrence kid. Rich. Obnoxious. Might have even deserved it."

"Well his pink Polo had a big red blood stain on it by the time we got him gone."

"I don't remember any of it. Was it late?'

"No, only about ten or so. I told you, you were in rare form."

"Tequila, Danny. Goddamn tequila. You know it makes me bark at the moon."

"You ate the worm again, too."

"Oh. Well. No wonder I punched someone then. Probably thought I was slaying a dragon or something."

Dan finished his beer. "Come on, Saint George. I want to get everything ready for the cold cut table before the waitresses get here. There's a new girl that I'd like to leer at suggestively, and I can't do that if I'm hauling roast beef and turkey breast up from the walk-in."

Sid drained his bottle, then put both empties in a case behind the bar. His head felt a little better now. But only a little. He hadn't expected it to do much, just take some of the edge off and wash a little of the barf taste out of his mouth. As they headed down the steps to the kitchen he looked at the time clock and realized that he hadn't punched in yet. He was reaching for his card when Dan said, "I clocked you in while you had your head in the garbage."

"Good man, you are."

The clock said it would be seven hours before his next beer. Sid sighed and opened the walk-in cooler, wondering, as he did every day, how he would make it till then.

THE EXTREME BUSYNESS of the day turned out to be a mixed blessing. On the one hand, Sid had to really drag himself through the first four hours of his shift, convinced at least twice that the sweet hand of death was coming for him at last. But at the same time it made the whole interminable seven hours pass by much more quickly than it would have if it had been a normal lunch crowd.

Hundreds of people who had been touched by Tom's music and gentle soul had come to the buffet. It had turned into a celebration, as people lingered long after their meals were finished, just to talk and laugh and cry.

Sid's experience of the event was less spiritual. He'd known Tom well, and would have loved to mingle with the people who had gathered in his honor. But it was his lot to remain in the dungeon, washing their dishes and running to the walk-in when the cooks ran low on burgers or chicken fingers. A few times Dan had called down to him to bring up more deli meat. Each time he'd gone upstairs, Sid noticed that Lane was looming there, frowning at him.

Lane Hazelton was a very wealthy man, having inherited a fortune from his parents, who had died several years earlier in a plane crash. Sid had tried to draw him into conversation many times, and had quickly concluded that Lane was, essentially, an idiot. But he somehow managed to turn everything he touched to gold. Maxwell's was one of four businesses that Lane owned, the others being a clothing store, an upscale burger joint and a Mexican restaurant just outside of town. All of them were thriving. And while it was no secret that Lane was very fond of his cocaine, he earned begrudged respect simply because he seemed incapable of failure.

Unlike most people, Lane did not particularly like Sid, and always seemed upset when he appeared on the first floor during his work hours. Sid was fairly sure that Lane felt that paying customers would be somehow offended by his appearance. Which was bullshit.

Granted, Sid had seen better days. The past few years of heroic self-abuse showed on his care-worn face. But he still made sure to shower regularly, shave daily, and visit Lucinda's Hair Salon once a month to keep his long brown hair from getting out of control. He did not look as bad as he felt.

Regardless, Lane had decided that sightings of Sid were bad for business. So he remained hidden as much as possible while on the clock. He resented Lane's treating him like Quasimodo, but he needed money and couldn't afford to lose his job. Better to remain hidden in the bell tower, so to speak.

And anyway, the shift was over now. Lane might own two-thirds of the town, but he didn't own Sid... at least not once he was punched out.

Sid closed the curtain of the tiny dressing room at the rear of the restaurant's basement level, nestled between the liquor locker and Lane's office. He peeled off his sweat-soaked and food-encrusted white shirt and pants, the official uniform of Maxwell's kitchen workers, and threw them in the over-flowing laundry bin. He pulled on his ripped Levi's and a powder blue sweatshirt, the arms of which had been cut off, then tied a navy-blue bandana over his curls and looked at himself in the dirty mirror that hung crooked on the bare drywall. Aside from a pair of rather dark circles under his eyes and crow's feet far too deep for someone his age, he looked presentable.

It was 4:30. This was Sid's favorite time of the day. Not only did it mark the hour at which his body finally felt free of the agonizing death-throes of his daily hangover, but it marked the beginning of Happy Hour, when he started it all again. Sid threw open the curtain and walked upstairs.

There wasn't much room along the highly-polished rosewood bar, as many of the people who'd come to the buffet had stayed to drink, resting their feet on the brass rail that ran along its base. But Sid happened to arrive just as a couple of women were leaving and he slid onto a high-backed teak barstool. Ron was tending.

Watching Ron tend bar was like watching Ali box. It was like reading Elliot. He was always in motion, but never missed an opportunity to talk for a moment to every customer. There was no cocktail he hadn't mixed. He'd even invented a few of his own, most notably the "Dr. Morgan," which was Captain Morgan's spiced rum mixed with Dr. Pepper. Sid had been amazed the first time he'd tasted one. It was perfect. Ron was also famous for never making a patron wait for a drink. Even the most crowded bar did not overtax Ron's poetry. He was, quite simply, born to be a bartender. And he proved it once again today, placing an ice-cold Labatt's Blue in front of Sid before either had said a word.

"May God bless and keep you always," Sid said to him as he took his first sip.

"How was Tommy's buffet?" Ron asked, wiping down the bar.

"I guess it went well. There were a ton of people. Lots of goddamn dishes. I brought Danny a fresh roast beef and the dining room was so full it looked like Parent's Weekend." Potsdam, being a college town, swelled in population when classes were in session, but never more than when the parents arrived for the school-sponsored visitation weekend. There were four schools in the area: Clarkson University and Potsdam State, and down the road in Canton there was St. Lawrence University and Canton ATC. During the three days that any of those institutions welcomed parents to prove that their money was being well-spent, Maxwell's was so crowded that Sid always pictured a cartoon building with its walls bulging and deformed because it was so full of people.

"Good. I hope we raised enough money to help Will pay down those doctor bills. Poor bastard."

Sid took another long drink then said, "Yeah. How much does that have to suck? First you lose your boyfriend, then you realize that his death has made you a pauper. God bless America."

Next to Sid sat an older man in a business suit. He was drinking Manhattans and he overheard what Sid had said. "Did you know Tom?" the man asked.

"Yeah. Tommy was great. He came in here a lot with Will. They were probably the happiest couple I ever met."

"That's nice of you to say. My name is Pete Sebastian. I'm Tom's dad."

Sid stood and put his arm around the gray-haired man's shoulder. "I'm very sorry for your loss, Pete." It was a spontaneous gesture, but it didn't appear to make the older man uncomfortable. On the contrary, it brought a smile to a face that had clearly been lately shaped by sadness. Indicating the crowd with a

25

sweep of his hand, Sid said, "As you can see your son was much loved."

Pete nodded. "Everybody loved Tom, ever since he was a little boy. He just had a spark, you know?"

Sid nodded. "Absolutely. He made you better for knowing him."

The older man turned from his drink and looked closely at Sid. "Thank you. That's very kind to say." He paused a moment then said, "You don't miss much, do you? You're a lot more impressive than your appearance would lead one to think."

Sid laughed. "I choose to take that as a compliment. Ron, would you get Mr. Sebastian another Manhattan please?"

As Ron set the drink down he said, "Yeah, don't let Sid's *Night of the Living Dead* look fool you. He's a genius."

"Shut the fuck up," Sid said, smiling none the less. Pete smiled again too.

The conversation went on for some time, leaving the sad subject of Tom and moving on to a wide array of topics. Ron, running from one end of the bar to the other, heard enough to catch snippets about politics, business, film, literature and music, all in a matter of twenty minutes or so. Sid got Pete laughing so hard at one point that he spilled his drink on his suit jacket. He excused himself to go to the men's room and tidy up.

When he left, Ron brought Sid another beer. "You're taking his mind off Tommy. That's good."

"He's a really great guy," Sid said. "Easy to talk to. Tom had a good dad."

As he took a drink of his beer, Sid felt a rather aggressive tap on his shoulder. He turned and saw that it was Lane. He looked angry.

"Sid, you can't sit here dressed like that and bother these business people. They don't want to look at you. You need to go."

For a moment, Sid had no words. Then there was what the long-abused wives standing over their bleeding husbands called a snap. He was suddenly overcome by a feeling that there wasn't much left to lose, and he turned and faced his boss. "You're seriously throwing me out of your bar right now? You're really doing this?"

"You need to go. This is a different class of people."

"Are you fucking kidding me? 'A different class of people?' Look, I'm sorry if my parents didn't have the good taste to fall out of the sky and leave me a boat-load of money like yours did, but that doesn't mean I'm some kind of sub-human. I've got just as much right as anybody to sit here and give you back the few lousy dollars you pay me. But you know what? I will go. You can stay here with your 'different class of people.' Maybe you can score some coke from one of them. Keep your bar, and keep your piece of shit job. I quit. Go fuck yourself."

"Nobody talks to me like that," Lane said, puffing out his chest like some bird preparing to do a mating dance.

"I just did, dick head. So by definition, you're wrong." Sid pushed past him. He considered making a bigger scene, maybe drilling Lane in the mouth, but then decided just to get the hell out. He left without looking back.

Sid walked across the street, toward the river. There was lots of green grass there, all of it bathed today in brilliant sunshine. It seemed like a less hateful place to be. He stormed for about a half mile along its bank before finally sitting down on the warm ground, facing the dark water that flowed past him, oblivious to his hurt and anger.

His thoughts swirled, and the gravity of the situation sunk in quickly. So now he was unemployed. Homeless, divorced and freshly jobless. He realized that he was not nearly drunk enough. Not nearly. Something needed to be done about that, and quickly. It was the one problem to which there was a solution.

He stood back up and retraced his steps back towards town. Pausing when he reached the sidewalk, he surveyed his surroundings. Potsdam was unevenly dissected by Main Street, which ran east to west, and Market Street, which ran north to south. The dissection was uneven because Main Street had buildings on one side only, the other touched the park. In spite of its name, Market Street was actually the "main street" of the village. It was lined with pubs, eateries, apartments, and shops.

Sid made up his mind. Instead of going left toward Maxwell's, and possibly not being able to stop himself from throwing a brick through one of the ultra-expensive plate glass windows that adorned the façade, he turned right and headed instead to Stan's Liquor Store, where he bought a bottle of tequila. "This is a good decision," he told himself, knowing fully well that It wasn't.

About the only thing anybody ever got arrested for in Potsdam was an open container violation. With so many college students walking its streets, proving that a good education didn't always impart good judgement, the small police department was kept busy enforcing its favorite law. Sid had no intention of ending up in jail. Not that it would have made things much worse. He just wasn't interested. So, he took the tequila, ensconced in its brown paper straightjacket, and pointed himself once more in the direction of the river. This time, in order to avoid incarceration, he hiked much further, going past the mowed green lawn, dotted with benches and littered with college students laid out on blankets. He hurried past the public area and ventured into the woods which formed the town's southern border.

The forest grew dense quickly. After walking for only a mile, in an angry straight line from the liquor store, there was no evidence of human life, save for Sid. And, at least to Lane's reckoning, Sid did not count as human life. Why was it so important to him that he make Sid feel small? What was it about him that bothered his boss – no, ex-boss, so desperately? Did kicking a man when he was down make him feel even more superior than he already thought he was?

Sid spied an especially welcoming branch about ten feet up in a sugar maple and, tucking the tequila in his pants so that he could use both hands, he climbed up and sat on it. Unscrewing the top of the bottle he took a long gulp. This wasn't going to be an evening of doing genteel shots with his friends. This was to be about emptying a very large bottle by himself and seeing where it took him.

It didn't take long for the distilled blue agave to start working its devilry. The truth of the matter was that tequila was never a good decision, at least not for Sid. Each time he took the mystic liquid journey back to Jalisco it ended badly. By the time the bottle was one-quarter gone, Sid could already tell that would be the case again tonight. But he did not stop.

It was a perfect June day, and the sun wouldn't set until after eight o'clock. The shadows were already getting longer, but there was a gentle breeze and the air smelled like childhood. So, Sid sat in his tree, comfortable. The darker the sky got, the more well-lit he became.

He thought about the people he no longer worked with at Maxwell's. Danny, P.B., and Scooter all worked with Sid in the kitchen and even when things got crazy during rushes, they always pulled together. Aside from Ron there was Don, Celeste and Dean serving drinks, and they all had taken care of Sid at one time or another. Likewise, most of the waiters and waitresses had treated Sid well, with one notable exception. There was a waiter named Dylan who was a few years younger than Sid. He had a mythological persona about him, as he'd left Potsdam a couple years ago, and had lived in Colorado for a short time. He came back with stories of epic adventures and amazing accomplishments. For some reason, everyone was very impressed by this. Sid didn't see anything that spectacular about any of it, but had kept his opinions to himself. It was Dylan who had, one night, while well into his cups himself, called Sid a loser. Until that moment, despite the downward turn his life had taken, Sid had never thought of himself as a loser. From that night forward, however, he was never able to think of himself as anything else. Today's debacle seemed to further confirm it.

When he'd drained half the bottle he began pondering what he would do once it was empty. Fall out of the tree, probably. But what about after that? "Seriously, Sid, what then?" he said aloud. Without any income he would not survive long. His friends tolerated his habit of crashing on their couches, but they certainly weren't going to feed him. One of the few perks of his job had been free food. And even though he'd nurtured excellent relationships with nearly every bartender in town, they couldn't slide him enough free ones to satisfy his bottomless thirst. He would not be eating or drinking in Maxwell's anymore, obviously. That bridge had burned and plummeted into a deep chasm.

By the time the bottle was three-quarters gone the edges of his vision were getting a little distorted. His brain seemed muddled and razor-sharp, simultaneously. Sid continued to weigh his prospects and became increasingly convinced that his future seemed very much in doubt. He'd been lucky to land the job at Maxwell's. The previous dishwasher had gone away to college downstate, and it was his personal intervention that had gotten Sid in. Prior to that he'd been a regular at the bar, and had played on their softball team, but he wasn't all that well known and Lane preferred to hire people he knew. It had been a stroke of good fortune that right when the job opened up Lane was out of town and it fell to the manager, Paul, to fill the vacancy. That had been two years ago.

Now he was quite well known. And that was bad. There wasn't any place else that was likely to take him on. Though he never missed a shift and when he wasn't getting sick he always worked his ass off, his love for booze and drugs was common knowledge. Too much of a liability, there would be no livelihood for him now.

By the time he finished the bottle and tossed it into the river, he was as drunk as he'd ever been in his life. But it was still not enough. He felt a burgeoning urge to do more damage. To himself, or to something else. Sid looked down from the branch. It hadn't been that difficult to climb up, but now he hadn't the slightest idea how he was going to get down. He vaguely remembered joking with himself about falling out of the tree a couple of hours before. That didn't seem so funny anymore. Likely, but not funny. After several minutes of drunken calculation, he swung a leg over the branch and attempted a controlled descent. He failed. As he laid flat on his back, watching the stars swirl around, he found himself smiling. "Looks like a van Gogh," he thought.

After a few moments, he was sure that he'd suffered no fractures, and found that he was a little disappointed by this. If he'd broken his neck his worries would be over. Even a broken leg might have done him in. He would have remained lost in the woods for days, eventually dying of exposure. *People don't die of exposure often enough anymore*, he thought. So if this wasn't going to be the place where he died, somewhere else had to be. He got up, brushed off a few leaves and twigs, and then started walking back in the direction of town. At least he hoped that was the way he was headed. "Should have left a trail of bread crumbs," he decided.

As he made his way through the undergrowth he continued to think about death. Then he began to think about *why* he thought so much about death. Melinda. That's what all this behavior was about. Even as he had entered new relationships, he never stopped mourning his marriage, yet another reason none of them lasted very long. Since Melinda had made it clear she was never coming back he'd been determined to end his life. But he was gutless and would never be able to do it quickly, decisively. Not in a manly way, like Hemingway.

By drinking as often and as much as possible, however, there was the chance of fatal cirrhosis. Or if he had an especially good night, there was always acute alcohol poisoning. But his tolerance was damnably high. That was part of the reason he'd started doing drugs. People died from cocaine overdoses all the time in Hollywood. Of course, they could afford a lot more blow than could he.

So, while there was no question that he wasn't doing himself any favors by maintaining his lifestyle, he simply wasn't getting to where he wanted to be fast enough.

Looking up through a break in the trees, Sid saw that the moon was full. He howled at it, just to prove a point. Jim Morrison had once sung of a brain that was "squirming like a toad." He understood that now. Something big was going to happen tonight, he decided. What that would be he didn't know, but it might just end up being the grand statement of his life. Or it might be the fulfillment of the death-wish he'd been nurturing since the day Melinda had walked out. *Probably that*, he thought as he stumbled over a fallen branch. *Most likely that.*

FORTY-FIVE MINUTES LATER, when he emerged from the trees onto the now artificially lit lawn of the riverside park, Sid could not shake the image of the revenge-bent gunslinger riding into town to shoot down the Dalton Gang. Once you got past the fact that he was walking, not riding, that he had no gun and that he knew no one named Dalton, the parallels were undeniable. He did have revenge on his mind. In the distance, he saw Maxwell's looming like a great sandstone Bastille. The three-story structure had been built in the 19th Century, as had been much of "downtown" Potsdam. It was indeed constructed of huge sandstone blocks. A year earlier there had been a tremendous thunderstorm which had torn the corrugated metal roof off the restaurant and had sent several of the large building stones tumbling to the street below. No one had been hurt, but one landed, satisfyingly in Sid's opinion, on the windshield of Lane's BMW. Or rather through the windshield. Sid had found Bird and they had rushed to her bathroom, laughing that this was the tornado for which they'd been preparing. They'd taken a long bath together, riding out the storm in style.

Maxwell's had been closed two weeks for repairs during which the staff all collected unemployment and partied on liquor and beer that had been looted by the janitor the night of the storm. His name was Stephen, but Sid called him "New Gary." He

33

managed to export enough booze to fuel several large get-togethers.

But the restaurant was open now. The swanky ceiling lights shone through the big windows as Sid drew near. He stood across the street, where the park ended and the village began, and stared at it for five minutes. Revenge.

But then he turned the other way and walked down the stairs from the street into Abel's Pub. Abel's was just about the only other place Sid liked to drink with any regularity. There were two additional bars that he sometimes visited: The Rusty Nail, which served two-for-one drinks on Wednesday nights, and Django's, which was the best place in town to hear live music. Muddy Waters had actually played there in 1983, just a couple of weeks before his death. But in general, if he wasn't at Maxwell's, you could find Sid at Abel's.

There were a couple of reasons Sid liked the Pub. It was much less pretentious than Maxwell's for one thing. Instead of a polished bar crafted from imported tropical hardwood, there was a great "U"-shaped mess, made of battered red oak and covered with the carved names of hundreds of patrons. Sid's engraved signature was on there, twice. Also, it had Ron, for whom it was a second gig. He worked there two nights a week. Compared to the stuffiness of Maxwell's, Ron found working at the Pub relaxed him.

The pub was owned by Abel Wallace, the only African-American business owner in the entire town. Unlike Lane, Abel adored Sid, and allowed him to DJ on Friday nights paying him twenty dollars and all the booze he could consume. For Sid, it was such a joyous task that he'd have done it for free. Or maybe just for the alcohol. Entertaining people with great rock and roll was the polar opposite of the soul-crushing grind of doing dishes. Abel spun a set of soul and funk tunes himself on Friday, from 8 to 10 p.m. before turning the mic over to Sid to rock the joint till closing. Each time Sid entered the booth, Abel would say, "Now it's time for Sid to come and play you an evening of Caucasian music." But Sid's style packed the place, causing Abel to love him even more.

However, twenty dollars a week was not enough to live on.

Tonight was Tuesday. At least it had been when Sid had walked into the woods with his bottle. When he opened the door and entered, he saw Ron behind the bar. Which meant it *was* Tuesday. Or Friday. In which case he was late for work. He looked at the DJ booth, which in his alcohol addled frame of vision was not behaving nicely, but rather was vibrating noticeably. No music was playing and Abel was not in there. Tuesday then, definitely.

"Where the hell have you been?" Ron asked as he sat down. There were five other patrons, all of whom were friends of Sid's. They waited to hear the answer to Ron's question. The story of his loud departure from Maxwell's had made the rounds.

"I went for a walk in the woods," he said.

"Alone?" asked Kenny, possibly the only other African-American besides Abel in Potsdam. Kenny also tended bar at the pub, three nights a week.

"No, Kenneth. I brought Jose with me."

"Who the hell Jose is?"

"Jose Cuervo. We sat in a tree. I made it out alive, but he did not."

Ron just looked at him for a minute. "You drank an entire bottle of tequila? By yourself?"

"I did."

"Good God. How are you still speaking English? Let me buy you a beer." Ron opened a Blue for him and set it on the bar.

"That's smart thinking," Kenny said. "Maybe it will sober him up."

As Sid took a drink from the bottle Ron said, "I know you had to leave after that fuck did what he did, but I wish you could have seen what happened after you booked."

"What happened?" Sid asked.

"Tommy's dad came back from the crapper and asked where you'd gone. Lane was still standing there, still fuming, and he was all, 'I threw him out. I'm sure you didn't want that kind of scum bothering you.' Well, Pete went up one side of him and down the other. He asked Lane what breed of idiot, specifically, that he was and told him that from the short time he'd spent talking with you he could tell that you were probably the smartest person that Lane had working for him, certainly the most compassionate and kind, and that Lane was, in no uncertain terms, a douche-bag. Then he tipped me fifty dollars and walked out."

"Are you making that up?" Sid asked.

"I swear before tiny baby Jesus it is the truth."

"You're right. I wish I could have seen that." Sid sat silently for several minutes, trying to decide if Lane's humiliation at the hands of a "respectable" patron was sufficient retribution for the way he'd treated him, not just today but pretty much every day since he'd started working at Maxwell's. "I think part of that fifty is rightfully mine," he said at last, not meaning it.

Kenny stood up and grabbed Sid by the shoulder. "Come on," he said leading him to the liquor closet. Abel's Pub was located in the basement of the Armistice Hotel, another grand sandstone structure that had once been the town's premiere lodging house. It had been converted to low cost studio apartments in the

1960's. The basement was actually a vast cavern, although the pub itself was relatively small. The liquor closet, however, stretched for hundreds of twisting feet and was the perfect place to smoke a joint or snort a line. Kenny insisted that they do both. They smoked first, because, per Kenny's logic, it would take the edge off Sid's massive tequila buzz. Passing the joint to Sid, Kenny said, "You should have punched the mutha-fucka in the face."

"Certainly thought about it. I'd already quit. What was he going to do, fire me?"

"I'da laid his ass out."

"I know you would have. No one messes with Kenny." Sid let the smoke out slowly and quickly felt the marijuana's calming hand on his brow. The tequila was still doing most of the talking, but he could hear the pot saying, "Relax."

As he was spreading the cocaine on the small mirror that never left the cavernous liquor closet, Kenny said, "No one messes with Kenny's friends either. I may fuck him up yet." He killed the first line and handed Sid a rolled-up dollar bill.

Sid snorted one, then a second, and then handed the bill back. "Don't bother with that prick," he said. "You'll end up in jail and he'll just open another restaurant or something." The blow quickly turned Sid's brain into a crackling, over-stimulated cesspool. The word "buzz" was kind of a trite staple of the booze and drug world, but when Sid did coke it became a very literal expression of what went on in his head. It felt like two rival hives, the Crip bees and the Blood bees, were fighting for control of what little was left of his mind, and It put back any edge that the ganja may have taken off and then some. They sat quietly for a minute, until he said, "I think I need another beer."

As they reappeared from the back room, Ron set them both

up, Sid with his brew and Kenny with a whiskey, neat. Sid sat back down and asked, "Ronny, do you believe in karma?"

"I do," he replied, "but you know, it seems to me that people like Lane are somehow immune to it. No matter how big a shit he is, everything just comes up golden."

"I believe in karma," Sid said, then added, "I have to, now more than ever." No one said anything after that for a very long time.

Everyone in the bar knew what Sid had been through in the past few years. They knew about Melinda waking him up to tell him she was leaving, then erasing every trace of having been part of his life within a couple of hours. They also knew about the two frightening months following her departure, during which he never left their apartment. Many of his friends came to visit him, but could not rouse him from his funk. There were entire weeks that Sid could not remember during that time. He had, quite literally, lost his mind.

And they knew that even after he had emerged from his self-imposed imprisonment, he was a different person. He went through the motions of living, but that's all he was doing. The "illusion of life," Sid called it when the chemicals made him philosophical. He languished, money running out, prompting his eviction from the last home he'd shared with his wife.

But Sid's friends were pretty much all drunks and drug addicts too. None were on any kind of path to success. So although Sid universally took his addictions to a higher level than any of them, they never thought to say to him, "Hey, man. You need to straighten out."

Rather they tended to say, "Have another beer."

It was getting close to closing time. Sid's bloodstream was so flooded with alcohol, coke and THC that it had finally rendered him virtually insensible. There would be no grand gestures tonight, no defining moments. Probably no fulfillment of the suicide dreams either. Just another night of fitful sleep followed by another hangover, a colossal one from the look of things. "Ronny, can I hit your futon again?" he asked as Ron began shutting the bar down. All the other customers, save Kenny, had already left.

"Of course you can. I won't be having sex with your old girlfriend tonight, so we can mellow for a while before you crash. Listen to some Floyd. Kenny's got some sweet blonde hash. You don't have to get up for work tomorrow."

Ignoring the part about Bird, Sid said, "That's right! I've got the day off. And the day after that too. All the days."

As the three men walked outside and Ron locked the door, Sid looked at the stairs that led up to the street. He knew that they couldn't possibly stretch for a mile into the sky, but that's what they seemed to be doing now. As Ron took his arm to steady him, he said, "I hate to ask, man, but what are you going to do now?"

"Try to walk up these stairs," Sid replied.

"Don't be a dick. You know what I mean."

"Yes I do, but I have no idea, Ronald. Honestly, my immediate goal is to reach the sidewalk. Once that's done, I'll walk with you guys to the apartment. Then I'll help Kenny dispose of some of his hashish. Nothing beyond that is clear. Nothing is coming to mind. I can't brain right now. I've got the dumb."

It took almost a full minute to climb the staircase, and when they had, Sid's head began to do some very strange things.

He started to feel very high. Of course, he'd already felt high, but this was different. He seemed to be getting more messed up by the second. If he'd been sitting down it might have actually been pleasurable. But he was walking between Kenny and Ron, and he was beginning to feel very unsteady. Then, as he looked across the street at Maxwell's, the red stone of the restaurant was suddenly replaced by dancing patterns which looked like spinning white lace doilies, somehow suspended in mid-air. They filled his entire field of vision.

He stumbled. Ron turned to look at him, just in time to see his eyes roll back into his head. Sid fell forward and landed on the concrete sidewalk, face first. Although the white lace had given way to blackness, at the moment of impact Sid felt a violent explosion and saw a flash of sickly yellow light. Then there was nothing.

FOR A VERY LONG TIME, there was only dark. No sight, no sound, no sensations at all. Part of his brain must have still been working though, because Sid felt a thought enter: *Death, at last.* Then Sid started to become aware of something else. It was the face of a woman. She was beautiful, with spikey blonde hair and the most perfect smile he'd ever seen. He had no idea who she was. He'd never seen her before. But as she continued to look down at him with piercing brown eyes and smile, he felt as though he'd known her for a long time, maybe forever. He wanted to ask her who she was, but he couldn't speak. She seemed to sense that he wanted to talk, and she held her finger to her lips, as if to quiet him. Then she smiled again and said, "It's time to come home. I'm waiting."

The next thing Sid sensed was Ron smacking him in the face and yelling, "Sid, wake the fuck up!" His eyes fluttered, then opened. "Holy fucking God!" Ron said. "What the hell, man? What the hell!"

"It's ok," Sid said. "This isn't death." Immediately he wished it was. His face felt as though it had been peeled away from his skull. He brushed his fingers over it, and his hand came away covered in blood.

"Don't touch it," Kenny said. "You're messed up, bad."

"Can you stand up?" Ron asked.

"I think so."

"Good. Do it. We need to get the hell out of here. Someone just went inside the deli to call the cops."

"Oh, Christ. Help me up," Sid said. As he stood, Sid realized to his amazement that aside from the screaming facial pain, he didn't feel that bad. Kind of tingly all over, but otherwise okay. He mind was enjoying a clarity that, given his intake of bad medicine, should not have been possible. They began walking away from the scene, pushing their way through the group of people that had gathered like vultures when he'd gone down. Once they'd put some distance between them and the now dispersing onlookers, Sid asked, "What happened?"

"Well, one minute we were walking, and the next you went all stiff and did a face-plant onto the side walk. The whole left side of your head looks like hamburger." Sid again touched his face, gently this time. Then he tried to adjust his glasses, as his vision seemed blurred, and discovered that the left lens was missing.

"Seriously, don't touch it," Ron said. "It looks like you've got bits of glass stuck in there. I'm going to try to clean you up." They arrived at the apartment a minute or so later. Kenny helped Sid sit on the couch, while Ron went to get some washcloths and a pair of tweezers. He then spent ten minutes pulling shards of shattered spectacle glass out of Sid's face. After he'd removed all that he could find, he gently wiped away with blood with the warm cloth. He gave the wounds a splash of hydrogen peroxide, which didn't hurt nearly as much as Sid expected it to, although it

41

did bubble up rather entertainingly. Finally, Ron dabbed some antibiotic cream on the cuts.

"That's probably the best you're gonna to be able to do," Kenny said.

"I want to see it," Sid said. "Help me to the bathroom." Ron once again took his arm, though he felt completely steady now, and led him down the hallway. Ron turned the bathroom light on for him and let him look into the mirror. Sid expected it to be bad, but not this bad.

While the right side of his face was unscathed, the left, on which he'd landed, was a mask of scrapes and cuts, very ground beef-like indeed. Jekyll and Hyde immediately came to mind. Two faces on one man. "I thought I was ugly before," he said.

Although it was obvious that Sid had suffered some sort of drug-induced seizure, the three of them decided that the best thing to do at that point was to smoke some of Kenny's hashish, and put Pink Floyd's "Meddle" on the stereo. Sid drew the smoke deeply into his lungs and held his breath. It made him feel better. When they'd left the bar, he felt completely out of control, but now he was calm, mellow, relaxed. He hurt physically, but not mentally.

When the record ended, he thanked Kenny and Ron for getting him to safety and for patching him up, and made his way back to the futon. As he flopped onto his back in the dark room, he thought about the woman he'd seen. It was obviously a vision brought on by his delirium. But, God, she'd been beautiful. And she said she was waiting for him. Waiting for him to come home.

Home meant Syracuse, or more accurately, Lafayette, a tiny rural community to the south of the city, much smaller and with far fewer bars than Potsdam. His parents still lived there. He'd visited them no more than two or three times in the past five years, feeling far too ashamed of his descent into madness to be in their presence.

Home. Would they accept him? Would they let him come back? There would certainly be better prospects for employment if he went back. He'd been gone since 1978, seven years earlier. No one knew him as Sid the drunk, Sid the addict. Anyone who knew Sid there remembered him as Sid the athlete, Sid the yearbook editor, Sid the poet.

Sid the guy who had everything going for him.

Could he be that again? Tonight he had come closer than ever before to dying – his main goal for almost three years. And now that it had almost happened, he wasn't so sure that's what he wanted anymore.

He had a college degree. He was even fairly sure he knew where his diploma was; under a chair at Bird's place. And though it would mean talking to Bird to get it back, maybe he could put it to practical use after all. Maybe in Syracuse he could parlay it into something resembling a real life. Maybe it was time to get the hell out of Potsdam.

He fell asleep dreaming about that smile, like something in a Lautrec poster but with none of the fin de siècle pessimism. "I'm waiting."

THREE WEEKS LATER, his face mostly healed, Sid and Ron threw Sid's few belongings into the back of Ron's red Chevy pickup and drove to Syracuse. Sid had called his parents the day after his "incident" and tearfully asked them if he could come home. He would only stay with them until he got on his feet, he'd promised. His father, with whom he'd had a rocky relationship all though his teen years, had shocked him by saying, "This is your home, Sid. You're always welcome here."

During his mending time, Sid had cut way back on his drinking. He'd considered stopping altogether, but after going a couple of days' cold turkey he began to get the DT's pretty bad. So, he had a couple of beers a night, which seemed to ward off the withdrawal, but still helped him keep his head mostly clear. He'd also refused any cocaine that he'd been offered, though he still relied heavily upon his marijuana. It made him feel calm and helped him to make, then not waver from, the decision to move on to a new phase in his life.

In fact, he and Ron smoked two joints during the three-hour ride from St. Lawrence to Onondaga County. He was pretty high when they pulled into his parents' driveway, but since that's how he'd spent most of his senior year of high school, his mom and dad didn't seem to notice anything amiss now. They came to the door when he rang the bell.

"Why the hell are you ringing the doorbell of your own house?" his father asked in his heavy Bronx accent. He extended his hand, and Sid shook it. His mother grabbed him, embracing him long enough for it to feel awkward. When she finally let him go, Sid introduced them both to Ron.

They unloaded the truck. Sid had lived in Potsdam for seven years, yet all his possessions had fit into two cardboard boxes. One was clothes, the other a couple of books, his retrieved diploma, and a dozen or so vinyl albums. It was all he had to show for the first phase of his adult life.

The meeting with Bird, though initially awkward, had gone better than Sid had anticipated. After he dug around under the blue over-stuffed chair and pulled the framed sheepskin out, they'd sat and talked for a while. Sid had apologized for what he'd done. He hadn't even said "allegedly done." There was no point in trying to plead ignorance now. It didn't really matter anymore. What they'd had was gone, doomed from the start, Sid realized. When he stood to go, she'd walked him out, kissed him goodbye, and then closed the door on their relationship both figuratively and literally.

Ron stayed for dinner, then prepared to head back north. Sid walked to the truck with him. "Well, I guess it's time for you to stop dying and start living, huh?" Ron asked.

Sid hugged him. "I guess it is. You saved my life, man. Thanks."

"Shit. You saved your own life. I just cleaned off your fucked-up face." They laughed. Then Ron got into the truck and drove away.

SID HAD TAKEN another crap job, this time as a nighttime boiler man at a local lumber yard. It was only to tide him over until he found something better, he promised himself. The boilers provided heat for the wood-drying kilns and had to be kept at a constant pressure, which meant feeding huge slabs of wood into them all night long. But he didn't mind the physical nature of the work, and he was alone all night with no boss glaring at him. There was a radio, and he spent a lot of time reading between the boiler's feedings.

When he wasn't working, he was hanging out with Mark. Mark was, like him, a Potsdam transplant who had also once worked at Maxwell's. He'd been one of Lane's favorites, but he'd left the North Country two years earlier when his parents, who owned a diner in the Valley section of Syracuse, had decided to retire. They'd given him the diner, and he'd flourished in his role as chief cook and boss. He'd found out when he'd called home and talked with his brother, who was none other than Stephen, aka New Gary, the janitor at Maxwell's who had stolen all the booze when the roof blew off, that Sid was now in Central New York. He'd looked up Sid's parents' phone number and called him that day. That had been a month ago.

Sid had almost completely stopped drinking now, aside from the occasional beer. He swore he would never drink tequila again. Mark was not much of a drinker, so that helped.

Tonight, they were going to a Syracuse Chiefs minor league baseball game. Sid reflected on that as they got ready to leave. Going to a baseball game. Instead of sitting in a bar all night. What a concept. "I have to make one phone call before we go," Mark said. "I'm hiring a new waitress." Sid half-listened as Mark dialed and told the girl that she had the job and could start the following Saturday, if she was available that soon. "Good," he said. "I'll see you then."

As they walked outside and got into Mark's brown Toyota, Sid said, "New waitress, huh? What's she look like?"

"Pretty enough, I guess. Her hair's kind of punky for my taste. You'll probably dig her though, you dog. Come for breakfast on Saturday and check her out."

"I just may," Sid said.

"Of course you will. You come for breakfast every Saturday. Because it's free and you're a cheap piece of shit."

"And you're the worst cook in America," Sid lied, smiling at his friend. They drove to the stadium, and Sid happily watched the game, keeping score in his program. He quickly forgot about the new waitress.

WHEN SATURDAY CAME, however, Sid woke up early and drove from Lafayette to the Valley. A new woman was a new woman. A challenge, an opportunity...who knew? At the very least he'd get breakfast out of the deal. He sat at the counter. It still seemed a little strange to him to sit at a counter and not order booze. "Do you want the special?" Mark asked.

"Yeah. So where is she?"

"Around," Mark said, drawing the word out, verbally inserting a lot of extra "o's". "She's working, so she's kind of everywhere." Sid's facial expression relayed that he was a little annoyed with Mark's evasiveness, so he added, "I think she might have just gone into the kitchen."

While Sid waited for his eggs, ham and toast he drank some coffee and watched the door by the cash register that led back into the kitchen. He didn't know why he was suddenly so mission-driven, so hot to see this new girl. For all he knew she had a boyfriend, and he was still working at the lumber yard, not exactly a major catch. He doubted she would even give him the time of day.

Then she walked into the dining room and Sid's jaw dropped. It was her. It had to be her. The beautiful girl with the blonde spikey hair and the perfect smile. So very much like the girl from the vision, or hallucination or whatever it had been. It was absolutely her. When he'd seen her that night on the ground in Potsdam, he'd only seen her face. He looked intently at that face now. The eyes might be shaped a little differently, but were still brown and quick. The line of her jaw might be a little more rounded, but the softness of it was alluring. The smile, though. The smile was exactly as he remembered it. And now, in the flesh, he saw that she had a smoking body to go with her flawless face. Bonus!

He couldn't believe it. Things like this didn't happen.

S. J. VARENGO

Certainly not to Sid. How could he have seen this face, this very face? It was like some Philip K. Dick novel. It just couldn't be real.

But there she was, and there he was.

He turned to the guy sitting next to him at the counter and tapped him on the arm. "See that girl?" he asked. The guy nodded. "I'm going to marry her."

"Sure you are, pal. Sure you are."

A short time later business died down and Mark called the waitress over and introduced her to Sid. "Kim, this is Sid. The most pathetic excuse for a human being you will ever meet."

She looked at him and smiled. Sid almost started crying, she was so beautiful. When she spoke, Sid was sure he was hallucinating again.

"Welcome home," she said.

"THE TERROR"

The night was not quite night yet. The braver stars were already on the clock, but there was still more than a little red washing the horizon. "You're not night," Ted thought, addressing the sky. "You're night's bitch." The headlights of his rusted blue Subaru didn't do much to illuminate the black strip of highway that bisected the desert, but aside from cacti and lizards, there wasn't much to see anyway.

Ted glanced at his gas gauge, knowing he'd guessed wrong when he didn't stop at the service station that was now an hour behind him. He and the Subaru had both been showing their age lately and neither of them got as far on an eighth of a tank these days. The radio oscillated between static and a faint signal from a Vegas station. It was during one of the moments when the signal was solid that Ted heard a sports radio show talking about the fight.

"The champ, Batan Muhammed, doesn't figure to have much trouble with Billy Joe DePaul tomorrow night. An easy defense for a hefty paycheck. The main support, however, which features Raul Hernandez against Ted 'The Terror' Simon, has the makings of a real beauty. Simon, who by all rights should be the one challenging…" The radio faded again, but it was enough for Ted. He smiled. It was not a happy smile.

After another twenty miles it was darker and the weak headlights were just mailing it in. Ted squinted. Fifty feet ahead the so-called high beams picked out the form of an animal on the road. From the looks of things, it had met rather abruptly with something in the other lane. Ted ventured a guess that it was the truck he'd seen a half hour earlier. It had been a beer truck, he remembered. Now the sight of the flattened animal made him thirsty all over again.

It was a little odd for a highly-ranked middleweight contender to be driving by himself from his training camp to the resort casino in which he would be fighting, but Ted had insisted. He wanted to clear his head, he'd told his manager. He passed a sign that said "Las Vegas – 75," and he looked once again at the gas gauge. The needle flirted obscenely with the big red E.

"No way," he said aloud, grimacing at once. His words hadn't broken the monotony as he had hoped. Instead, they rattled around the interior and reminded him that he was alone.

He'd been alone since the night eight months earlier when he'd fought Billy Joe DePaul in The Garden. He had just finished up with the flu, be he never backed out of bouts. His KO punch had probably been flushed away, along with his diarrhea, but he didn't figure he'd have any trouble out pointing DePaul, who was only a so-so puncher with a wide-open door for defense. The first six rounds had been all his. His jab was almost invisible, it was so quick, and it was flustering DePaul to no end. His combinations were crisp and the straight right, though not really doing any damage, was scoring, easily and repeatedly. In the fifth frame, he'd trapped DePaul in the corner and landed a right uppercut that had bounced Billy Joe's head back. The ropes burned a spot between his opponent's shoulder blades.

Between rounds, rather than listening to the instructions from his trainer, Cally Lambert, Ted was looking down to the ringside seats where his wife Marilyn was sitting, next to his childhood friend, Terry Adams. As children, back in Brooklyn, Terry had predicted that Ted would one day be world champion, and that he would write about it. Terry had made quite a name for himself as a sportswriter at the New York Post, but Ted had not become champ. Not yet.

A victory in the Garden would guarantee him a crack at Batan Muhammed. He looked down hoping to see appreciation or at least confidence in his wife's face. Instead, he saw unmasked anger. He began to think more about Marilyn and less about the man in the ring with him.

Because of this, he wasn't careful in the seventh, and he let Billy Joe butt him good during a clinch. The referee, Hank Pearson, (who Ted always called "Head-Up-Ass" Hank), missed the butt completely, allowing himself to be screened by DePaul's body. He did, of course, see the powder-puff left that DePaul placed in the general vicinity of the cut about twenty seconds later. Any moron could see that the punch couldn't have cut through an overripe avocado, but Pearson stopped the action and had the ringside doctor look at it.

The doctor, who Ted's trainer referred to as Frank "Fear of Blood" Belzer, dabbed at the cut with a piece of gauze and said, "It's bad."

"It's a scratch," Ted said. "Besides, da mother-fucker butted me."

Belzer ignored Ted and turned to Pearson saying, "Stop it."

Ted was furious, but not worried. After six rounds, if a fight was stopped because of a cut caused by a butt, they went to the scorecards. He figured they'd give him a technical decision because he was so far ahead at the time of the clash of heads. But the wheels of the politics that Marilyn so loathed were turning. DePaul was declared the winner by TKO at 1:06 of round seven.

When Ted looked again to where Marilyn had been sitting he saw that she had left. So had Adams. He hadn't heard from either of them since.

Ted tried hard not to think about Marylin. It did him no damn good at all. He struggled daily to put up a wall around his brain through which she was not permitted. Training for a big fight on the Strip, one that would be broadcast on pay-per-view to millions of people, was tough enough without dealing with thoughts of his estranged wife. But once the image of Marylin clawed its way through his mental defenses, as it always did, he found it impossible to think about anything else.

They'd first met when Ted was still boxing as an amateur. Ted was a typical Brooklyn boy and had learned his skills both in Armenson's Gym on Wyckoff Avenue and, just as often, on the surrounding streets and alleys. It was not far from the gym that he'd first come upon Marylin's radar in a most dramatic fashion.

Ted was walking home from a particularly rough workout when he saw a group of three toughs on the corner of Stockholm Street and Irving Ave, giving the business to the most beautiful woman he'd ever seen. Even from half a block away, Ted could see she was tall and slender, built like a swimsuit model, and clearly in distress. As he got closer he could hear them assailing her with lewd remarks. When their catcalls and gutter remarks evolved to grabbing and groping, Ted stepped it.

"Leave her go," he'd said calmly. He was anything but calm. His arms, tired from an hour on the heavy bag, felt like hanging meat at the sides of his body. He wasn't at all sure he could lift them, let alone use them. One of the guys, a stocky Puerto Rican fellow who had about six inches and fifty pounds on Ted, let go of Marylin's arm and turned to face him.

"What you gonna do, hero?"

Ted looked from him to the other two guys, a scrawny white kid, and a lanky black dude, who had Marylin's other arm still tightly grasped. Ted saw the fear in her eyes as she looked at him pleadingly.

"Well, I'm first going to break dat asshole's arm unless he leaves go of the lady," he said pointing to the tall kid. "Den I'm going to hit da skinny guy on the right side of his chin with my left hand. Den I'm going to beat you, widdin inches of your miserable life, I tink."

However, before they could process any of his bravado, Ted flew instead at the big guy. He'd known, even as he was explaining his battle plan to the hoods, that he'd have to take care of the puertorriqueño first. He was the only real danger. So he led with a left hook and followed with an uppercut. The thug fell like the sack of turds that he was, and with his leg twitching in a manner that the other two toughs found very disturbing, just laid there. Before Ted could turn his attention to either of the other two, they began to run, exactly as he'd hoped they would, because there was no way he was going to be able to lift his arms a second time.

"Oh my God! Thank you so much!" Marylin said. "I thought they were going to kill me." Ted couldn't take his eyes off her. She looked like one of those girls in the Macy's ads, blonde with green eyes that smiled even when her mouth wasn't. Her nose turned up slightly, a trait that had always appealed to Ted for some reason. Her neck was long and slender and all he could think about was touching her there, letting his fingers gently trace along the smooth skin.

"Prob'ly not," he had told her. "But I doubt dey were going to ask to buy you ice cream." She laughed, and he laughed with her, lamenting it at once, as his bruised ribs screamed. He winced and touched his side. Marylin noticed.

"You're hurt," she said. "But those boys never even touched you!"

"Not them," he answered. "I got a whole team of guys who get to punch me every day over at Armenson's. I'm a boxer."

"A pretty good one too, I'm guessing," she said, pointing to the still unconscious guy at their feet. Ted listened to her voice like it was music. She sounded sweet, educated. Not like Ted, with his thick Red Hook inflection.

"Yeah, about him… We might wanna make light of dis place before he wakes up. I don't tink I could do dat again right now. Standing around here, it ain't prob'ly such a smart idea."

"So, what do you think we should do?" she had asked, showing him for the first time the mischievous smile that would reduce him to a powerless baby for the next ten years.

"I guess I could buy you some ice cream," he said. "Since dey ain't gonna."

The graphic visual memory of that first meeting, and of the abandoned seat in Madison Square Garden ten years later both dissolved now, and the bleak desert landscape returned to the fore of his consciousness. In the shallow distance, a solitary building could be distinguished. Ted looked a third time at the gas and said, "Fumes don't fail me now." The echo of the empty car made him mad again, but his anger retreated as the small shack turned out to indeed be a tiny gas station. Ted pulled in, heaving a sigh of relief, and looked through the picture window that comprised a controlling percentage of the front of the building. He saw a grizzled old man, who he immediately named "Pops," motion for him to pump his own fuel. He filled the tank and went inside.

Over the armrest of the beat up old chair from which Pops showed no sign of moving, was a Ring magazine. It was the issue with Ted on the cover. He was always a little squirrely about being recognized. Ted's stomach tightened without warning. But instead of the wide eyes of adulation, Pops' eyes, he saw, were a little misty. He took Ted's American Express and pointed to the TV screen where Bogey and Ingrid Bergman were ripping each other's hearts out for the zillionth time in "Casablanca."

"That's what happens when you fall in," Pops said. "Damned if they don't stick it to you in the end. Had me a wife what couldn't understand how a man could be proud of a place like this." He made a take-it-all-in sweep of his left hand while sliding the card through the reader with his right. "Called it a pile of shit. She called it a dump." Ted noticed that the air was permeated with the smell of pungent blackberries and caught sight of an empty brandy bottle lying on its side like a sleeping lover, next to Pops' chair. "She didn't know a damn thing about what happens to a pile of shit when you sweat on it. Didn't know a damn thing about how a diamond and a dump is the same thing once you take a bullet in the arm, just before you swing your pipe and crack open the punk's head rather than open the register. Didn't know a goddamn thing."

Ted's gut had a red-hot rivet nesting in it as Pops handed back the Amex. He didn't need this right now. It was stomping on all too ragged nerves. He didn't need it, but Ted realized that Pops did. For a guy who made his living messing up other people's faces, Ted had always been empathetic. Their eyes locked and Ted nodded slightly. It was the only movement he could muster. Finally Pops said, "Worse thing a man can do is love a woman. Sooner or later, she'll kill you."

"Ya know, dere's a football game on the other station, Pops. Maybe dat...instead of dis?" Ted said, not realizing till a second later that he'd used his made-up name, but it didn't seem to bother the old man. He just smiled a tiny smile and dabbed at the corner of his eye with a grimy handkerchief. He reached for the remote and changed the channel.

Ted felt as though it was alright to head out now, and he opened the door. Just before he stepped back into the night Pops said, "Watch out for that little Mexican bastard's left. I saw him take out a guy with one swipe last year. Get to his chin quick. Okay?" Ted grinned a tiny smile of his own and nodded.

He climbed back into the Subaru and made it the rest of the way to Vegas without thinking of Marylin any more than ten or fifteen times.

- - -

The ring was twenty feet square, but Ted knew they'd use very little of it. Neither man was a dancer. Hernandez couldn't go lateral if they tied ropes around his waist and yanked him, and Ted only moved when he had to. He didn't figure he'd have to with Raul.

Hernandez was a tough character from Zapopan, Mexico, a city of over a million people that no one in the States had ever heard of. His record was 25-8. That spoke volumes. Twenty-one of those wins were by KO, the result of that left hand that Pops had warned him about. So there was no questioning his power. But the eight losses made a statement as well.

The Bellagio was full, even though the main event was still over an hour away. The people all knew that Ted "The Terror" should be fighting Batan Muhammed for the middleweight title in that main event, even if the World Boxing Federation didn't want to admit it. The raucous crowd was going to see Muhammed retain his title in the main event tonight, but the real reason they had come was to see Ted the Terror flirt with Rockin' Raul's left hook. This had to do with Ted's popularity and the fact the promoters had emphasized Hernandez's punch and not his questionable jaw. In truth Cally Lambert and Ted's manager, Al Angati had picked Raul as a "safe" opponent. Ted's punch wasn't as good as his, but almost. His main advantage was that he had power in both hands. Hernandez had that left hook, but his right was feeble. What's more, as The Ring had said in that cover piece about Ted, "Not since Jack Johnson has a fighter been able to score so well and shut an opponent down so total-ly." It went on to say, "The only fists that ever get through his guard are those thrown by his wife, Marilyn, when Ted forgets to take out the garbage." The article had been written by Terry Adams.

As the microphone was lowered to the ring announcer, Ted realized that he was once again damnably distracted. Instead of focusing every gram of hate and fury in his body upon the chin of Raul Hernandez, he was scanning the ringside seats for a glimpse of Marilyn. He saw happy faces, expectant faces, the faces of diamond encrusted woman and black tie sporting men. But he didn't see her face.

In the years since that first meeting on a Brooklyn corner, Ted had seen that face every day as they built a life together. When Ted had won the Golden Gloves and then when he had gone professional, Marylin was at ringside for every bout. After the fights she tended to his cuts once they were stitched, and she rubbed liniment into his tired muscles. And she was in his bed every night.

But gradually things began to change. Nine years as a professional boxer was like fifty years to most people. The human body wasn't designed to be constantly pounded on and even for a fighter as skilled defensively as Ted, a toll was taken. His love for Marilyn never wavered, but she had come to realize that even though she wore his ring, she would always be the other woman. For Ted, the Sweet Science was his first love.

For most of those years, years characterized by months in training camps, followed by a flurried night in some ring in New York, or Atlantic City, or Chicago, or many less well-known locations… for most of those years, Marilyn was acceptant of her place in Ted's life. It hadn't taken long after the night he'd rescued her for the realization to dawn upon her that everything in their lives together would rotate around the brutal sport.

But the truth was that she hated everything about it. She hated the time away from home when Ted was in training. She hated seeing him get hurt. Though his career had been marked with far more success than failure, the fight game was one that paid its participants primarily in pain. He'd made enough money to purchase them a lovely home in Long Island, but they spent far too little time there and as Ted had climbed up the rankings,

Marilyn had gradually come to resent the very thing that had brought them together.

Just before the DePaul fight, she'd been cooking them a pot of chili. Even though he was a top middleweight contender, Ted still liked to train at Armenson's when he was going to fight in New York, so it took an hour to make the commute from Brooklyn to the Island, and when he'd called her to say he was heading home she'd started putting the ingredients together. But as the spicy chili began to heat up, she got to thinking about Al Angati's promise that this fight would be the one that would finally get Teddy the title shot he'd been working so hard for. She'd heard Angati say that more times that she cared to remember. Al said it and said it, over and over again, but the title shot never materialized. And Ted refused to see the truth. By the time the chili was boiling, so was Marilyn. When Ted walked in a short time later, she was looking for a reason to let loose on him. As he dropped his smelly gym bag by the door, it was all she needed.

"Jesus, Teddy, that thing stinks. Why do you have to bring that stench into my house?"

Instead of taking the bait, Ted picked up the bag and set it out in the garage. "Sorry, Mar," he said as he came back in.

"Sure, You're sorry. You're always sorry, but you always do it. Nothing ever changes!"

"Baby, what's goin' on? Why you all pissed at me?" he'd asked, confused and hurt.

Finally, she could hold back no longer. "The ring, Teddy. That's what's wrong. The goddamn ring! I'm so sick of it! So sick of the bruises and the cuts. So sick of you not letting me hug you because your ribs hurt too much. I'm sick of the promises and the lies and the bullshit, Teddy!" She burst into tears.

He'd tried to put his arms around her, but she pushed him

away. "But baby," he'd said. "We're so close! Dis fight in the Garden's gonna be on HBO! When I beat dis punk, dey gotta give me Batan. I'm one fight away from bein' champ, Mar! Don't you see?"

"Don't you?" she'd screamed at him. "Don't you see that Al keeps on telling you that? That this fight is going to be the one, no matter which fight it is? And that every time after you win and come home to me all banged up, he calls and says, 'You know, Ted. It's the politics. The WBF picked someone else to challenge. Next time, Ted, next time.' Don't you see?"

He'd said nothing after that. He went to the kitchen and filled himself a bowl and sat by himself at the dinner table. After a while Marilyn had come and sat too, though she didn't eat and they didn't talk. That night as they lay in bed, Ted thought about how Cally had been drilling him to keep DePaul on the ropes as much as possible. Marilyn thought about thought about ropes too. About reaching the end of them.

At last the strong baritone of the announcer's voice brought Ted's attention back inside the ring. He listened to Hernandez's build up. "In the blue corner, to my left, weighing in at one hundred fifty-nine and one-half pounds...originally from Zapopan, Mexico...now training out of Los Angeles, California, with a solid record of twenty-five wins, eight losses, featuring twenty-one knockouts, wearing the red trunks with gold trim, 'Rocking' Raul Hernandez! Hernandez!" There was a fair amount of cheering, a few boos, but mostly just the buzz of apathetic conversation as the crowd showed minimal support for the Mexican fighter.

Then the announcer said, "And in the red corner, to my right..." The crowd went wild. It was doubtful that anyone aside from the TV audience could hear as he continued: "Weighing in at one hundred sixty pounds, from Brooklyn, New York, with a record of fifty-eight wins, four losses, two draws, with forty-seven knockouts, wearing the solid black trunks, Ted 'The Terror' Simon! Simon!"

The referee, Lou Grosch, was a veteran. Competent, fair, but slowing down a bit, he gave his instructions in a crisp tenor. "No low blows, no rabbit punches, fighter scoring a knockdown go to the furthest neutral corner." Hernandez glared at Ted, but he gazed beyond his foe, towards ringside. Grosch continued, saying, "Obey my commands and conduct yourselves as professionals." In Ted's mind that had always meant the same thing: "Forget everything I just said and try to kill each other."

He went back to his corner where Lambert slipped in his mouthpiece and said, "You can end this in the first, Teddy. Put him out and there's no way Batan can duck you anymore." Ted didn't even bother to nod. At that moment he didn't give two shits what Batan did. It was what Marilyn did that concerned him. If Cally had any inkling of how far Ted's mind was from the ring he'd have had a coronary. Yet when the bell rang he shuffled to the center of the ring, muscle memory taking control.

But right away he knew something was wrong. Hernandez's guard seemed much more authoritative than it did in any of his fight films. The hours of screening that Lambert and Angati had crammed down his throat had shown a complete numbskull who was prey to anybody who was just tall enough to reach above his belt. But *this* Hernandez had his chin tucked squarely on his chest. The right hand was held at shoulder height, and the left flicked out in the form of a jab which was not only measuring Ted but scoring on him as well. This really pissed him off, and being angry in the ring is almost as bad as letting your focus slip to the crowd. Being angry and being distracted? That was a death wish.

After Raul's third consecutive jab snapped his skull back, Ted's concentration improved somewhat. He remembered that he knew how to throw punches as well. Taking a quick step to his left, he dug a right into Raul's ribs. As he expected, his guard dropped just the amount that instinct called for and his chin moved about an inch. Ted threw a left hook and found that an inch was just enough. His bright red glove raked across his opponent's jaw and the bones in Hernandez's legs seemed to dissolve.

Ted moved quickly to the neutral corner, and immediately began to look into the crowd, still believing that Marilyn would be there. For him. He somehow still believed that the vehemence of his dream was enough for the two of them. He still believed that the championship would make all the frosty, silent nights they'd spent together melt away. So intent was he on finding her and so sure that Raul was finished, that he didn't hear the count stop at eight, nor did he hear Grosch bark the command "Box," after he'd wiped the resin off the gloves of Hernandez. Ted didn't hear, but Raul did.

Hernandez had beaten the count and now he saw Simon breaking the cardinal rule of the Sweet Science. Ted had forgotten to protect himself at all times. He had his back turned. Raul rushed him and landed his infamous jack-hammer left … to the base of Ted's skull. It was a completely illegal punch, but that mattered little now.

The blow caused an explosion in his head. He saw the stars that he'd always thought were merely poetic exaggeration. He didn't feel himself hit the canvas but was eventually aware that he was no longer standing. He sensed a tickling spot of warmth on the right side of his head, which was, in fact, a trickle of blood issuing from his ear.

The referee pulled Hernandez off.

Now Ted's eyes were working only some of the time. He had managed to roll onto his back and he saw a doctor standing over him. The doctor's head looked strangely simian. Then he saw nothing.

Then he saw Angati and Lambert moving in slow motion toward him. They were engulfed in flames. Then he saw nothing.

Then, in the blue corner, in the red trunks with gold trim, he saw Marilyn, her gloves lifted high, sweat dripping from her naked breasts and her curly blond hair. She was smiling her mischief smile.

And even as his eyes stopped working once again he heard the ring announcer, sounding as if he was speaking from a million miles away, say, "Winner by disqualification, at 2:01 of the first round, Ted 'The Terror' … the Terror … the Terror."

And then there was nothing.

SHE CAME TO ME AGAIN LAST NIGHT

"She came to me again last night," David said.

I didn't answer him. He knew I wouldn't. What could I say? What is the correct response when your best friend informs you that his dead wife has visited him? No ... visited him *again*.

Again was the key word. He'd broached the subject with me the previous week, as we'd sat in the dimly lit confines of Patterson's pub, and had begun to drink our fourth Tanqueray and tonic of the evening. Patterson's was an oasis of old-school style in a world of corporate sports bars. There was still just one TV, an ancient CRT model, on a shelf behind the bar built specifically to hold it. The channel selection was controlled dictatorially by Ed Patterson, himself an oasis of old-school style. It was our safe place.

Him talking about it that night seemed to have been less difficult for him that one might imagine. To be fair we were, after all, already three T&Ts deep, and I was feeling no pain, as they say.

But whoever "they" were, they couldn't say the same for David. He was plenty drunk, alright, but since Cara's passing six months earlier he was in a constant state of pain.

But gin and pain make strange bedfellows, and he just blurted it out.

"I saw Cara last night. She came into the bedroom and watched me sleep."

"If you were asleep, how did you see her?"

"I'm speaking metaphorically, douche," he said.

"Ah." I figured that pretty much put the topic to rest. She hadn't *really* come to him. She was a metaphor for his loneliness and suffering. I supposed it was a worthy tribute to have been made into a metaphor.

But that's not what he had meant at all.

"She didn't actually watch me sleep, because I was awake."

I'm probably not the most astute guy in the room, even in a room that didn't contain any gin. This one did, though not as much as when we'd arrived, and I wasn't yet attuned to the seriousness with which he was presenting this information. I decided to slough it off with some humor.

"And how much gin had you consumed before bed?"

David frowned. He looked at me as if he couldn't understand my failure to immediately accept what he was saying at face value.

"No gin, Drew. No gin, no beer, no nothing. Well, coffee, actually. I had two cups of coffee before bed while I was going over a brief."

"Hmm, Caffeine late at night can effect your perceptions too."

"Andrew!" he shouted loudly enough that a few heads turned in our direction and Ed Patterson gave us the stink-eye for interrupting his enjoyment of the Mets getting slaughtered on TV. He continued with less volume, but no less intensity. "It was not any chemical actin upon my nervous system. It was Cara."

TONIGHT, as I had that first time in the bar, I stopped talking and just looked at him.

Between the night at Patterson's and now tonight in my man cave, as I called, not inaccurately, my entire house, he'd told me about her coming three additional times. Each time, apparently, it was the same. He lay in bed, not sleeping, and she stood nearby and watched him not sleep. The flat screen was flickering, providing little more than mood lighting as we both ignored the baseball game we had, ostensibly, gotten together to watch.

I still wanted to believe there was an easy explanation: too much to drink, or David being exhausted, as he often seemed to be, even now, half a year after losing her. Either was a viable answer, but neither, he insisted, was correct. So I had stopped offering opinions. I'd stopped the first night, but that didn't mean I'd stopped *having* them. My current one was that my friend had suffered a nervous breakdown, and was regularly hallucinating. But there was something about my hypothesis that bothered me.

He never saw anything that wasn't really there at any time other than bedtime, and no place other than his own home, in his own bed. I am not a psychologist, and I suppose there are many forms of mental sabbaticals. But I watch a lot of documentaries, and I have never heard of any that occurred in only one setting. He never saw anything when he was with me. Or at least he never let on.

The other problem with my theory was that he seemed to be perfectly rational with regard to every other aspect of his life.

He'd gone back to work, started going with me to Patterson's again... started *living* again.

But if I'm being honest, he seemed pretty rational about this as well. Apart from the complete, absolute absence of there being any such thing as ghosts, and the fact that Cara was snuggly interred in a marble crypt paid for by her father and mother, next to an empty one reserved for David, which he'd paid for himself. I knew goddamned well that she was there, because I, along with three of Cara's brothers, David, and Cara's dad, had carried her coffin from the funeral parlor, where we had all shared a tearful farewell as David slowly, painfully closed the lid, at which time we carried her coffin to the hearse, and then had taken it from the rear of the long black limo of death to the crypt. We'd ridden in the car directly behind the hearse, so I'd have known. I'd have known if she was making good some cruel prank, sneaking off only to appear at regular intervals as David lay in his bed, grieving her. Because an absolutely world-class, albeit evil prank could be the only real explanation.

So sadly there was, despite his continued calm, almost detached description of her visits, no way of explaining her appearances.

Since the beginning when he told me about it he was completely unruffled, composed. As he spoke now, it was the same.

"She was wearing her favorite jeans. The ones that didn't fit for a while, but then did again," he told me.

This was almost beyond "calm and detached." This was borderline cold. Because the period during which Cara's jeans stopped fitting was when she'd really begun showing. She lost the baby soon after, which was why her jeans fit again. His almost cavalier description hit a nerve I guess. Maybe if I'd had a handle on any part of what he was saying, I might have called him on that. But I figured it might be his way of being able to talk about Cara, to focus on that pain by glossing over the pain of losing the baby.

"And she had a white blouse, light and gauzy. It seemed to be fluttering, like there was wind. But we were in the bedroom."

A flurry of dismissive questions, which I knew that I would never ask, flashed through my head. *Was the air on? Did you have a window open?* But I suppose imaginary women's imaginary shirts didn't care whether there was really a breeze or not. An imaginary breeze was more than sufficient.

"Her hair was blonder than at the end. It was light, like when we came back from Italy. Do you remember?"

I remembered. They'd taken a trip to Europe the autumn after the baby, and in preparation Cara had gotten her hair, naturally a chestnut brown, lighted several shades. During the month long trip she'd visited a salon in Venice, and had come out completely blond. David had liked it very much. That night they'd made love on the roof of the hotel under the Italian stars and David had allowed himself to believe that everything was going to be alright. Yes, they'd lost their baby, but maybe they might conceive a new life in that magical setting.

But when they'd gotten home, Cara's knockout new hair color in tow, he sometimes caught her wincing for no apparent reason. Although she never complained the pain became more frequent, less easy to ignore, and impossible to mask. When there was more pain than not she finally went to the doctor, believing that there might have been some complication from the miscarriage. Something like that. Something fixable.

Instead they were told it was ovarian cancer, and that it was very aggressive and very advanced.

She'd fought it like a trooper, submitting to every horrible procedure that the doctors had ordered, all in hopes of beating it, at first, then later of adding just a little more time. But finally she had refused any further treatment because, she said, she wanted her own hair for her funeral. She ended up having enough time for it to grow back into short curls in her natural brown.

Then time ran out.

"Do you know what really gets me?" David asked, snapping me back to the present.

"What?"

"I can smell her perfume."

Before I could stop myself I asked, "Don't you still have a bottle of it in the room? Maybe you smelled ..."

He cut me off, not angrily but emphatically. "No. It's gone. Everything is gone. I went a little crazy one day and just raced through the house, getting rid of everything that reminded me of her. The perfume was one of the first things to go. I donated all her clothes to Goodwill and took down all the pictures. I gave her dad all her books and I just made believe that she'd never existed and that I was miserable just because that's what I am. A miserable prick."

"When was that?" I asked, wondering if it was recent enough for a hint of the scent to linger.

"The day before she came for the first time."

I had my turn at an irreverent thought then. *Maybe she was pissed at your for getting rid of her shit.*

But I stopped asking questions at that point. Instead, I took a sip of my beer. Never for a minute, a second even, did I entertain the thought that hearing about this experience was harder for me than it was for him to actually live it, but it was pretty damn hard nonetheless. I'd known David since junior high, where he was the first kid that talked to me. I'd fretted all summer long about that, because moving from Detroit to a rural town in Central New York was pretty much everything the text books described "culture shock" as being. We weren't the only black family in the tiny burg, but I was the only black kid in Morton Beamer Junior High School, and that scared me, despite my supposedly being the big city tough among the throng of rubes. Truth was I wasn't tough at all, and some of the rubes were pretty damn big. But I had worked like hell to give off that urban aura. David, of course, had seen through it, asking me on the second day of school if I like Marvel comics better or DC. Of all the things he could have said, he picked the one thing in the universe that I was passionate about. I launched into a fifteen-minute diatribe on the merits and the shortcomings of both publishers, all seemingly without drawing a breath. His response sealed the deal.

"You just talked for a quarter of an hour and didn't answer my question, dipshit."

That had made me laugh, and we'd been best friends pretty much from that moment.

So, yeah. Hearing him talk about this insane experience in his completely rational manner was plenty hard enough. At first, when I was still holding out hope that he *had* been sleeping and it *had* all been a dream, that it would be a one-time thing, it really didn't shake me that badly. It would be a one-time occurrence, I reasoned.

The second time he talked about it was a little worse. By the fourth time I would have begged him to shut the hell up if not for … everything. If not for his months of suffering. If not for his conviction about what he was saying. Now he was on about it again tonight and I really wanted—*needed*—for it to stop. I'd like to say that I wished for him to be free of this pain, but the truth was that I didn't want to have to worry about him anymore. I didn't want to sit uncomfortably, listening to the crystal-clear detail of it all, to the infinite certainty with which he spoke. I didn't want to agonize over what, if anything, *I* should do. Did I need to intercede? Did I need to grab him and drag him off to King's Park Psychiatric Hospital? Did I need to get in his face? To scream at him and tell him to knock his crap off?

These were questions for which I had no answer, and I was not inclined to work through them, at least not at the moment. I grabbed us each another beer from the cooler, situated strategically between out two recliners. I twisted the cap off of mine, but he sat for several minutes, his bottle unopened, staring at the TV but, I knew, not seeing it. He was seeing her in his mind, as she'd appeared to him the night before. Beautiful, blond, not ravaged by cancer. Alive. Or not. Jesus.

After a few more minutes he handed the beer back to me, still unopened, and said, "I think I'm gonna head. I guess I'm not into baseball tonight."

"That's fine, dude," I answered, standing. I walked with him up the stairs to the front door, gauging his steadiness as we went. He'd only had two beers, spread over the course of the entire evening, so I wasn't too concerned about his sobriety. But alcohol wasn't the only source of potential instability.

When we got to the door he turned to me and said, "I need to be there for her if she comes."

I felt this was a crucial moment, one in which if I said the right thing, maybe he'd turn a corner, right the ship. Maybe he'd be okay, or at least start down that path. But I had nothing, so I just nodded.

"Alright, I'll call you tomorrow," I managed.

"Yeah," he said absently, already walking down the steps to his car.

I walked back inside and bolted the door. After a moment's consideration I turned back to unlock it again. What if he needed someplace to go in the middle of the night? But then, realizing that I'd had six beers in the same time it had taken David to drink two, I left the latch alone. He had a key. Just like I did to his house.

Like I did to his house.

Before I had time to think, even to fully realize what I was doing, I was behind the wheel of my pre-owned SUV. I'd driven three blocks before something resembling common sense caught up with me.

"You're buzzed," my conscience said. "Buzzed driving is drunk driving."

"And you can just shut up," I said aloud. "He needs me."

Common sense was not done having its say, however.

"He needs sleep, not a midnight visit from his drunk best friend."

"I *am* his best friend," I said, prolonging the conversation. "This is what best friends do."

About then it occurred to me that having an audible conversation with an inaudible voice inside of my head might be almost as crazy as Cara visiting David from beyond the veil in the dead of night. That thought actually made me chuckle, much to the chagrin of my slighted common sense.

David's house was, mercifully, only a five-minute drive from mine. Five minutes and one world apart, I often joked. It was at the rear of a very nice cul-de-sac, along with other lovely homes filled with very nice people who weren't particularly interested in other people arriving for a visit in the middle of the night. My headlights illuminated David's house. I had just retrained myself to say "David's house," and not "David and Cara's." I'd managed to go a whole day without saying it for the first time a few weeks before she stated her nocturnal drop-by's.

His was a larger and far nicer house than mine, (thus the "world apart" crack), but David had done much better for himself than I had, in just about every regard. It was he who cracked the top ten in our high school class, at number four. I was a dismal number eleven, just a shade below the elite, but which he repeated told me was "still damn good." I have remained unconvinced of this all these years. It was also he who, after we both got into Columbia, which *was* damn good, even I admitted, who used it like NASA uses the Kennedy Space Center, as a launch pad. He joined the frat, he graduated Summa Cum Something-or-Other, and he met the woman of his dreams. I tended to just scrape by academically, pouring my real energy into frequenting the drinking establishments of Morningside Heights, especially those that featured live blues music. Not that David didn't crawl with me from time to time, but let's just say his plate was filled with richer, more savory food than mine. It was David Allen Coe who passed the bar two days before marrying Cara and who, by the time their fifth anniversary rolled around, had made full partner at his firm, while Andrew Steel Smithson went to work for a non-profit which, like most non-profits, provided much better for its clients than it did for its staff. At night, more and more frequently alone as David settled into the life he had blueprinted for himself when we were still kids, I would pound out short stories, a few of which I actually sold under the pen-name "Smithson S. Andrews." I thought myself incredibly clever.

So David owned a house worth over a million dollars, while I lived in a much less affluent neighborhood, in a much less impressive house, which I rented. Just barely rented, if I'm being straight with you, because there were still months when making the life-tariff was in doubt.

I killed the engine as I pulled into the driveway. His car wasn't visible, but he used his garage, so that didn't throw me. What did cause me a pause however, was that that front door was ajar. It wasn't wide-open, so I didn't notice until I was about to slide my key into the lock, but it was definitely not shut tight and secured.

I thought he might have taken the trash out and forgotten to shut it afterwards, but I didn't notice if the cans were by the arcing curb, and decided not to turn around to check. I just hoped it was something that pedestrian that had led to it being left unlatched. I pushed it open a little more. Just enough to peek in and whisper "David! It's Drew!"

No answer. Clearly he was out of whispering range.

Opening the door fully, I stuck my head inside and looked around. There was no sign of anything untoward, so I entered and quietly closed the bright blue door behind me. David and I had both always thought the door color was something of an abomination, but Cara had anguished over it for days, looking at paint swatches piled high and page after page of online catalogs before selecting just the right shade of electric blue and dubbing it "Perfection." We both loved her too much to disagree openly.

There was utter silence shrouding the house. When we were kids, David's parents had owned a big grandfather's clock, and when he and I would sneak in after our curfew you could hear that ticking, even if there was no other sound. No sound, that is, until his dad flipped on the light next to his chair and said, "Damn it, you two. What is so difficult about the concept of ten o'clock?"

In the age of digital clocks there is no ticking. There was nothing at all to disrupt the sepulchral stillness.

As a result my footsteps on the ceramic tile floor sounded like bombs going off.

"Jesus!" I hissed, angry at myself for not removing my shoes as soon as I came in. *Buzzed walking is drunk walking*, I chided myself, certain I heard my common sense chuckle. God, I hoped it was my common sense I was hearing. I took them off now and carried them in my hands as I moved toward the (thankfully) carpeted staircase, with its long, polished wooden railing. I don't know if looking at the railing effected David the same way it did me, but it always made me a little lumpy in the throat because I remember when they bought the house, Cara had said she couldn't wait until little butts were sliding down the railing. Obviously, none ever had.

I started up, avoiding the fifth step, which creaked, and wondered why I was being so stealthy. I suppose I thought that if, in fact, David had managed to climb into his far-too-big-for-one-person bed and pass out, I didn't want to wake him. His mind and body needed all the restorative magic they could glom onto.

Or maybe I was hoping not to disturb Cara.

"Jesus," I said again. What the hell? Where had that thought come from?

In all the spectral visits that David had described, Cara had never spoken. She just stood there, her hair and blouse flowing in a wind which was, apparently, just as spectral as she. She stood and watched him, watched *over* him, he'd said. As if she merely wanted to assure herself that he was all right. As if she needed to keep him safe.

As I neared the top of the stairs I felt as thought *I* was the one who needed to be watched over, as I got a little unsteady just before reaching the landing. I almost did a comical, slapstick ass-over-tea kettle roll back down the entire flight of stairs, perhaps becoming the next ghost to confront David after dying of a broken neck. I caught myself on the railing at the last second, and looking at my hand tightly grasping the shiny wood, I felt bad all over again for the little butts that never were.

The hallway at the top of the stairs held five doors. Four went to bedrooms, and one was the guest bath. David's (*just* David's ... not "and Cara's"), was at the end of the hall. The room I had always crashed in when spending the night was the last door on the right. It was, officially, the guest bedroom. Unofficially it was Andrew's room. On the left wall were the kids' rooms. They had never gotten around to furnishing them. Cara had lost the baby early enough in her pregnancy that they were still more concerned with whether or not to ask the baby's gender at her next ultrasound. The ultrasound that never happened. As a result the nursery, which was the room closest to the master, was completely empty. The other bedroom, to which their oldest would have graduated when their second child came along, was full of boxes. At least it had been prior to David's decision to empty the house of everything that had Cara's touch upon it. A lot of those boxes had been filled with her stuff; old textbooks, photo albums that she never got around to digitizing ... things like that.

All the doors were closed except David's. I tip-toed down the hallway, still carrying my shoes in an act of courtesy which was lost on the circumstances. The only person in the house was the one I was about to call out to, and that made the furtiveness somewhat moot. As I neared the door I whispered, "Dude! It's me!"

From within the bedroom I heard him chuckle.

"No shit," he said. "What's the matter? Couldn't sleep? Do you need me to read you a story?"

I stuck my head in and saw him sitting up in bed, still fully dressed, eating boneless chicken wings out of a green bowl and watching Jimmy Kimmel. He patted the mattress next to him.

"Sit down," he said, holding the bowl slightly aloft. "I made too many."

Some people might be put off by the sight of two men in their thirties stretched out on a bed together, eating Anytizers. Major trigger for the homophobes. But we'd been crashing at each other's houses in each other's beds since seventh grade, and we really didn't think much about it. Even Cara had gotten used to it, though she'd always insisted on being in the middle. "If anybody's gittin' any from this boy, it's gonna be me," she'd say, and all three of us would laugh. Every time.

Now it was just us two, again. And nobody was laughing, even though Kimmel was hilarious, as always. We laid there for a while, cramming spicy chicken into our food-holes, only snickering a little now and then as Jimmy and Matt Damon went at it again in another round of their famous pseudo-feud.

Finally I said, "So … quiet night so far? No … company?"

"Just you, asshole," he responded, not taking his eyes from the TV.

"I meant *besides* me. You know what I'm talking about."

"Of course I know. I guess I've gotten used to you thinking I've lost my mind, but I didn't really expect you to come by and check on me?"

"Really?"

"No, not really, dolt. I knew you'd show up sooner or later, if only to be on hand to sign the commitment papers when they came to take me away."

"I don't think you're crazy."

"Not even a little?"

"Can't lie. Always thought you were a little bat-shit. Even before all this. Way before all this. Always, like I said."

"Screw you."

After that we didn't talk for a while. I suppose reading that you might think he was pissed at me, but this was really pretty standard for us. The better the insults the happier we were, and the silence was mainly just time for thinking up the next zinger. Eventually the vat of chicken was gone, and we threw what seemed like about two hundred soiled paper napkins into the bowl, which he set on the nightstand.

The musical guest was performing, some singer-songwriter kid that I'd never heard of, and who didn't impress me a ton. I asked David if he knew anything about him, but when he didn't answer I glanced over and saw that he'd fallen asleep. Good.

I debated trying to climb off the bed and leave him be, now that I was satisfied that he was alright. But I knew he was a light sleeper and that as soon as I moved I'd wake him. So I stayed put for a while, and when Kimmel ended I grabbed the remote, which was laying between us in Cara's spot, and I switched off the TV. I closed my eyes.

After what seemed like just a minute or two I felt a chill, as if a breeze was coming in through the window, so I opened my eyes and looked. The window was closed tight. I turned to look at David to make sure he was still sleeping. He was.

And standing next to the bed watching him was Cara.

She looked exactly as he'd described her, as she when they'd taken their trip. I literally had to remind myself to breathe, not because I was frightened, as I should have been. No my breath was stolen by her incredible beauty. Her blond hair was indeed being ruffled by a zephyr I could feel, but which had no source. The flowing edges of her sheer top also undulated. Her eyes bore down upon her sleeping husband.

I inadvertently made a sound. Not quite a word; something between a grunt and a name. When I did, Cara seemed to notice me for the first time. A smile warmed her face. She held up one finger, and wagged it back and forth in a "naughty boy" gesture. I knew what she was saying. If anyone was gittin' anything from him, it would be her. I almost expected her to climb over David's sleeping form and wedge herself between us, but she just stood there. After a moment her attention moved back to David, and there it stayed.

After watching her stand by the bed for what seemed like an hour, I began to have new thoughts. I wondered, now, that it he'd only seen her on five nights because those were the nights he hadn't been able to fall asleep. I wondered if she'd been there every night. Then I wondered if that might be why out of the few weeks he had been talking about her visits he'd only had trouble sleeping five times. Maybe her presence was the reason he could sleep at all. He'd talked more about *not* sleeping far more often before she'd ... returned.

I was also aware of and amazed by the fact that I was completely unafraid in the presence of what I could call nothing other than... the ghost of Cara Coe. I had never believed in anything like this. I'd laughed at psychics and passed on Ouija board sessions when we were kids. I figured there was enough weird stuff right here in the everyday, and I didn't feel the need to seek out the supernatural.

But now I was being confronted with it, undeniably. And it was fine.

She seemed totally content just to look at him. She never

reached out to touch him or moved to sit on the edge of the bed beside him. Other than her teasing hand gesture towards me she didn't really seem to move at all, aside from the other-worldly fluttering in the non-existent wind, and her eyes blinking occasionally. I got the feeling she preferred not even her own eyelids interfered with gazing at the man she so adored.

I now had a new theory. I reasoned that, for whatever reason and by whatever means, she had chosen to remain. All their hopes and dreams had been taken from them, and yet somehow she managed to overcome what I assumed were some pretty restrictive barriers in order to simply be with him, to watch him sleep, as he'd said the first time he told me.

Eventually I found myself so weary that I could no longer keep my eyes open. With a final glance at her slightly luminescent form, I drifted reluctantly off to sleep, content to be the three of us together once more. My last thought was of telling him in the morning that I believed him, that I'd seen her too. That it was all real, and somehow it was all okay.

WHEN I DID WAKE UP, the sun was already blazing through the window, which for some reason was now wide open. Putting my arm across my not-quite-ready eyes, I heard a bird singing outside, and for some reason that sound brought the memory of last night came to the fore of my consciousness, and I rolled over to tell David what I'd seen.

He wasn't there.

David had always been an early-riser, all part of that over-achieving, Type-A side of him that had driven him to such success. So I thought nothing of his absence. I flopped onto my back and lingered for a few minutes before hauling myself upright. It was a Thursday morning, and I had my own obligations to think about as well.

I was just about to leave the room when I noticed the sheet of paper on the bed where David had slept. I picked it up, assuming he'd left me a not telling me I was a lazy bastard and would never amount to anything if I didn't start getting up earlier to face the day with a breath of fire.

Instead I found these words in David's steady script:

She said, now that you knew I wasn't crazy, that it was okay for me to go with her. There's no need to worry about it, Drew. It had to be this way. Without her there was just no point. But for her to come back, so many times, it was obvious that I need to go too. I'm gonna miss you buddy, but at least now you know that the end is not really the end, and eventually the three of us will be able to crash together once more, with her in the middle, of course.

Be good,

David

I felt cold, suddenly, and sick. There wasn't much room for alternate interpretations. I'd never read a suicide note before, and sure as hell never held one in my hand, but I recognized what I was holding was exactly that.

I raced out of the bedroom and began throwing open all the doors on the second floor. He wasn't in any of them. I flew down the stairs, taking them two at a time and hitting the creaky fifth one dead on. I called his name, even though I was beginning to fear he wouldn't answer. Couldn't answer.

I must have looked as though I *was* the crazy one as I dashed from room to room, eventually running into the garage, fully expecting to find him there, as it was the last place in the house I hadn't already looked.

His car was there, but he was not. Not slumped over the wheel in a cloud of carbon monoxide, not hanging from the metal rafter. He was gone. Just … gone.

I went back inside and sat heavily upon his micro suede sofa, and put my feet up on the glass-topped coffee table, a habit that Cara absolutely detested. She'd swatted my feet dozens of times, with whatever she had in her hands at the moment. I feared no retribution now.

I sat for a long time, trying to decide what the hell to do. Finally I pulled my cell out of my pocket and made two calls. First I called work, and told them I wasn't coming in. Then I called 911.

The operator was a little condescending. From the description I had given there was no indication that anything was wrong, other than the note and the fact that his car was still here, but he wasn't. Eventually I was able to convince her to dispatch a patrol unit. The two uniformed officers were just as skeptical, even after I showed them the note and tried to explain what he meant by his dead wife coming for him. "It's the nightmares, you see?" I told them. I didn't say a word about the previous night. Didn't want anything to do with what they'd think of that. Me getting hauled off to King's Park wasn't going to do any one any good. Well, not me anyway.

As the day went on, after calls had been placed to David's office, his dad's house and to all of Cara's family, the authorities began to take his disappearance a little more seriously.

Eventually they told me to go home, but no further. I had never occurred to me that they would think I was somehow involved, but now I realized that I was the most obvious "person of interest." Hell, I was even black!

After a couple of days, when David failed to reappear, everyone began to take it all *very* seriously. I spent several hours in very unpleasant conversation with the detectives at the Suffolk County Sheriff's Department, but as there was simply no evidence that I'd done anything, or really that anything criminal had even been done at all, I was eventually released.

A week went by, then a month. When no trace of my friend had been found after a year, most people stopped thinking about it. The authorities would give me a call from time to time, asking if I'd heard anything—probably making sure I hadn't gone anywhere, in case something *did* turn up.

For the first few weeks of that year I was convinced that my friends had gone somewhere, and without leaving a trace of evidence behind, had ended his pain the only way he could think of—by ending his life.

But as more time passed and there was no evidence found to support that theory I began to wonder.

I had never doubted what I'd seen that night. Oh, believe me, I *wanted* to have doubts. I wanted lots of them. I wanted to believe I'd stayed asleep and dreamed the whole thing. I wanted it to be a side-effect of eating boneless chicken wings then passing out without properly digesting them.

But I couldn't. Not really because of what I saw, but because of what I'd *felt* that night when Cara came to him again. The peace that washed over me as I watched her watch him, the peace that lingered, even during the turmoil and chaos of the ensuing days... that was a gift from her, I believed then, and I still believe it now.

So now I have to think he had somehow been able to, as he

said in the note, just go away with her. Stupid, I know. Freaky, bizarre, pick your own descriptor. But after that night, the things I thought impossible could no longer remain so. The things I thought didn't happen in the "real world" had happened in front of my eyes, but more importantly, within my soul. And if the things I saw were true, then maybe the things he wrote were as well.

And so now, as I sit at my kitchen table in my so-much-less-wonderful-than-David's-house house, writing down these final words, I'm left with two dichotomic feelings. On the one hand, I live know that there is a love so strong that not even death could hinder it. On the other, as I towel up the beer I just spilled on the table while trying to write this story's end, I'm more than a little jealous that my best friend, the guy who never missed a beat, the guy who almost had it all, ended up with such a love, and I ended up spilling beer on these scant few pages which I was able to fill to tell this tale.

But there's a swallow left in the bottle, and I raise it now to David and Cara.

THE CARDINAL

The water in the tea kettle made it rock on the burner when Jake set it down. Click – click – click. He had burned his hand, for the hundredth time, on the black Bakelite handle when lifting it off the flame. The oven mitt sat six inches away, untouched. "Every damn morning," he said aloud, but under his breath.

Despite the pain, there wasn't really room for anger. Making tea for Beth was his church service. He approached the task reverentially, assembling the elements as carefully as the celebrant prepared the host. Sugar, half and half, two tea bags. She had him add turmeric because she had read that it was an effective natural anti-inflammatory. It gave the brew a ghastly yellow tinge, however, as though the tea was jaundiced. Which was ironic because turmeric also was supposedly good for jaundice, not to mention bloody urine, menstrual difficulties and flatulence. Beth didn't have any of the first three problems, and it had proven miserably ineffective on the last. The final ingredient was a dash of black pepper, added after all the others had been stirred together. Jake supposed it made the over-all flavor just a little less disgusting.

Jake had once seen a doctor who came highly recommended for pain management. After a soul-bashing initial consultation, which had been conducted by a panel of six physicians, each one's shirt slightly more stuffed than the one before, and all of whom Jake was sure were thinking that he was faking the pain, the so-called treatment had commenced in earnest. It consisted of one hour psychotherapy sessions which had nothing to do with his twenty-year relationship with a back that never stopped hurting. A young psychologist initiated the session, then the alleged wonder-worker would come in. While he was all for mental health, Jake was quite sure that his back pain was not related to how he felt about his parents. He grew increasingly angry at each appointment. Choosing a passive-aggressive approach, the more the two therapists confronted him, the less he talked and when the three-week program came to an end he shook both of men's hand and left without a word. But in his mind, he had broken both of their necks. The only suggestion related to pain relief they had offered in the entire course of therapy was drinking hot water laced with turmeric. He'd tried it for three days before abandoning it as quackery. Very bad tasting quackery.

But Beth embraced it. And so each day began with Jake faithfully combining each ingredient, like ancient Flamel fermenting the Philosopher's Stone, then carefully walking it to her, mindful not to spill any on the cream colored carpet.

Jake was a coffee man. He drank it out of a ridiculously large mug, into which he splashed a hint of creamer before pouring in the rich, dark brew, allowing it to mix the half and half itself as it filled. It was a trick he'd been shown by the director of the counseling center at which he'd interned as an undergrad. "This," the man had said demonstrating the auto-stirring technique, "is why I'm the director and you're the intern." Jake had been doing it for almost thirty years now, but had never himself become the director of a counseling center. Apparently, he concluded, there was more to it than just making your coffee stir itself.

As he sat next to Beth on the sofa she took a sip of the tea. "Mmm," she said. "It's a good cup." Another part of their daily mass; the beginning of the liturgy.

"Good," he replied. "I'm glad you like it." He took a drink of his coffee, saying nothing but basking once again in the feeling that a transfusion had commenced. Then they sat in silence for several minutes. On the television, Matt Lauer was speaking slightly sanctimoniously about some topic or another. They always turned on the Today Show, but never really watched it. Beth was still pissed at NBC for dumping Ann Curry, who she considered far more sincere than Savannah Guthrie. Beth called Savannah "snippy." They both liked Al Roker, however. He'd once been the weatherman for the CBS affiliate in Syracuse, and had gone to college in nearby Oswego. They'd called him "Big Al" back then. He'd sported quite the afro in his local news days, Jake recalled fondly. So Al was "theirs." Everyone else they pretty much just tolerated.

But the Today Show was none the less a key part of the daily mass. Jake continued to work on his coffee. Because his mug was so much larger than Beth's he always drank at a faster pace, in order to finish about the same time she did. He'd then head back to the kitchen to fix their second cups. While the teapot was once again warming up, Jake would open the vertical blinds on the sliding door that led from their living room to a small concrete veranda.

It was spring time in central New York, which meant that while it was over sixty degrees yesterday, there was three inches of wind-whipped snow outside today. Still, it was sunny and there was a cardinal sitting in a tree watching them watch him. Beth had heard that seeing a cardinal meant someone from heaven was visiting you. She believed it was her grandmother, who had raised her and who had loved Jake from the first day Beth brought him to meet her. Jake smiled when she said that, but in his heart, he hoped that if the whole visitor from heaven thing was true, it was Lou Gehrig in the tree outside, not Nonny. He'd loved Beth's grandma, but come on! How cool would it be if was the Iron Horse flying around out there!

Jake, having remembered the oven mitt this time, brought the two cups and sat back down. He'd been resting only a minute when there was a knock at the door.

This never happened. No one came to visit them, especially not at eight-thirty in the morning. It was as if the church service had been interrupted by a horde of Cossacks, kicking open the cathedral portals and storming down the nave on horseback. Jake set the coffee on a leopard-spotted coaster and opened the door. Outside was a sheriff's deputy.

"Are you Jake Duggin?" the young officer asked.

"Yes," Jake replied, undecided as to whether he should panic.

"Your brother is Ted Duggin?"

"Yes," said Jake, quickly starting to make up his mind.

"I'm very sorry, but your brother has passed away."

Jake was sure the cop had just punched him in the gut, but could see that he hadn't moved. "Ted? My little brother is dead?

Are you sure? He's only forty-two." Beth had come over and put her hand in the small of Jake's back.

"What did he say?" she asked.

Jake turned to her, his eyes rapidly filling with tears. "Teddy died," he said. He turned to the deputy again. "What happened? Was it an accident?"

"No, sir. When he didn't show up for rehearsal and didn't answer his phone, one of his band mates went to his apartment. He knocked but got no response, so he went to the window and looked in. Your brother was on the floor.

Jake knew without asking that it would have been Will who'd found him. They'd been playing together for years, in a series of bands that never enjoyed much success. For Ted, it was never really about making it big, though. It had been about the absolute love of music. Jake was eleven years older than Ted, and had introduced him to the Beatles when Teddy was just a little guy. They had both inherited the love of music from their mother, who had made sure that both of their lives had a soundtrack. Jake sang and played a little guitar, but it was Ted who had the talent. He'd started his first band in high school and had never looked back. No matter what else was going on in his life, there was always music.

Will loved music too, but his real devotion was to Ted. In his eyes Ted could do no wrong. He'd followed him from one group to the next, always letting Teddy make the decisions, just happy to be part of whatever he was doing. Jake could only imagine what had gone through poor Will's head when he'd peered through that kitchen window.

"So you don't really know what happened yet?" Jake asked.

"The M.E.'s people are there now. They're ... removing him," the deputy said. He continued to talk for a while, but Jake wasn't really hearing him. Beth's hand, rubbing his back in a vain effort to comfort him, felt foreign, detached. If he just believed hard enough that none of this was real, maybe it wouldn't be. A mistake. An incredibly cruel hoax. Anything. Anything.

But it *was* real. After talking to him for a moment more, the deputy handed Jake a card with the medical examiner's phone number and told him to call later that afternoon. "By then they might be able to tell you something," he said. "Again, sir, I'm very sorry."

"I know," Jake replied, taking the business card. "Thank you." He didn't really know of the man was sorry or not, and the last thing he felt like doing was being thankful. He closed the door and collapsed into Beth's arms. "Teddy's gone," he said, "he's gone!"

They stood by the door for a long time, Jake crying and Beth whispering to him. "I'm so sorry. I love you. I'm so sorry." Eventually she was able to lead him back to the sofa and she helped him to sit down. Still weeping, he sat slumped over, his head in his hands. Thoughts spun wildly in his head. Images formed, uninvited. Teddy as a baby. Teddy on his prom night, dressed in a white tux, Jake and Beth serving as chauffeurs for he and his date in Jake's badass '77 Cutlass Supreme, Ted on stage singing, his bass slung low, his long hair tinted red by the lights – a look of pure bliss on his face. Around the memories whirled, like timbers from a shattered house in some private tornado.

Jake became aware of Beth's hand on his knee. He lifted his head and looked at her. He was about to thank her for just being there when he heard a tapping sound. He turned to look out the glass doors. Sitting on one of the folding chairs they kept on the veranda, was the cardinal. As Jake looked it tapped the glass with its beak once more. Then it turned its head at an angle, as if viewing Jake quizzically, wondering why he looked so upset. After the briefest instant of connection, it flew away.

He said nothing, but for the first time felt a kernel of fragile belief in something at which he'd always scoffed. He stopped weeping, and lay his head on Beth's shoulder.

A DELIGHTFUL DISTRACTION

Nicole Jacks looked at her watch. Then she swore, turning so that the light of the streetlamp by which she stood shone more directly on its face. And on the many diamonds that surrounded its face. Then she swore again.

"Dammit, this is a pretty looking thing, but I *cannot* tell time with it." She pulled it closer to her eyes, fearing for a minute that she might be noticing a hint of deterioration to her vision. But the watch was clearly in focus, the numbers were just too damn small.

Doesn't matter, she thought. *He's late. I don't need a twenty-thousand-dollar piece of junk to tell me that.*

Behind her, the glass and metal door of the Western Wine Bar opened, allowing a wave of sound from the band—Don't even get me started on this band, she thought—to gush into a still warm evening in early autumn.

The Western was generally considered a quiet place, which is why Nicole had suggested it to Guillermo. But tonight, there was a band, rendering it well into the "anything but quiet" end of the spectrum. And Guillermo was late.

The people who had come out of the restaurant were a couple in their sixties. The man held the door for his wife, who looked at Nicole as she walked past, then shook her head slightly, her eyes looking sad, in a compassionate way. "Pity," she said quietly to her husband.

Nicole turned away from the couple, her face falling into darkness as the streetlamp cast her shadow on the sidewalk. She was smiling. The woman had taken her for a jilted woman, waiting for a date that was, at best, only running late. So sad.

Nicole was, of course, anything but.

Still, the prick *was* late, and she was hungry. As the door swung shut again, she was grateful to it for containing all but the thudding bass of the band on the other side. But she was also conscious of the fact that, band or no, she needed to get inside, get some dinner, and charm the sox off Guillermo as she probed for his weakness.

She opened her purse. It was slightly larger than the clutches preferred by most women her age. At twenty-six, a bag this large *could* lead an observer to think she might be one of those mothers who started having babies right after high school, and had clearly already given up.

But one look at her put that impression to rest. Everything about Nicole Jacks, from the top of her tall and heavily sprayed blond hair to the pointed tips on her red stiletto heels, screamed that she was a young woman looking for fun. It was an image she had carefully cultivated, and she pulled it off with such perfection that a slightly enlarged handbag wasn't going to make much of a dent in the impression she made. She turned slightly to allow a bit of lamplight over her shoulder and into the bag's interior.

Pushing the Sig Sauer P228 out of the way, she found what she was looking for.

She opened the compact and turned again to face the light, using the mirror to see if her makeup had eroded since she'd applied it several hours earlier. Aside from a stray eyelash she looked fine. As she flicked the renegade lash away, she heard footsteps drawing near from behind and she altered the angle of the mirror. A tall young man, dark complexion made even more so by the shadows from which he was emerging. His hair was dark and wavy, and so laden with product that it shined in the streetlight. She quickly closed the compact, made sure the pistol was positioned for easy access, and snapped shut her purse.

"Guillermo!" she squealed as she whirled around and fell into his open arms.

He hugged her warmly, but, she had to admit based on the absence of any protrusion as their bodies pressed against each other, not much *real* heat. "I am so sorry that I am late."

Nicole pulled back, though she still held his arms in her hands. She smiled up at him. His English was quite good. Far better than he realized, she knew. That's why he tended to enunciate very clearly, and rarely used any contractions in his speech.

"I should be very mad at you," Nicole said, faking a pout. "You are late and I told you when we talked on the phone…"

"That you were very hungry. Yes, I know. And as I said, I apologize most sincerely. It was a last-minute and very unavoidable… work thing."

Nicole smiled again, giving the impression that all was forgiven. She was actually grinning at the irony. An "unavoidable work thing." He *was* her work thing.

"It's okay. Let's go in. I hope they didn't give our table away. I told them you'd be along any minute."

Guillermo pulled the door open and Nicole saw his eyes blink involuntarily as the beat pulsating from the band, now unhindered by the double glass, hit him. She leaned toward him as she walked through the door. "I forgot to tell you," she shouted. "They've got a really good band tonight!"

THE TABLE NICOLE feared she might lose was the most strategically placed in the entire restaurant. Not only did it face the door, but thanks to an odd architectural decision, it was tucked in the corner of two walls which served no other purpose than, apparently, to provide a corner in which to place the table. And although she knew there was actually a narrow walkway behind the wall, Nicole also knew that this was used by staff only. It wasn't fool proof. The wall kept her from being seen from behind, but it wasn't going to slow a bullet down appreciably. Still, she factored the risk as being low. She knew the place well, knew the staff. She knew the layout of the kitchen, and therefore knew someone could *in theory* come in via the kitchen door and force their way through to the walkway in the rear of the house, and fire several shots through the flimsy barrier. She dismissed the threat knowing that anyone who could pull that off would have to know the place as well as her. Hell. He'd have to know *her* as well as her.

She smiled over her shoulder as Guillermo pulled her chair out. He moved to his seat, and Nicole noticed that while he took the seat directly across from her, he turned it slightly. She must have looked confused.

"I am sorry, Bethany," he said to her, using the name she'd offered earlier that day. "I mean no disrespect to you by angling my seat like this. I wish to look only into your beautiful eyes. But I have recently suffered a minor injury to my back, and turning like this reduces the pain. I do not want it to distract me during our wonderful evening." He smiled, and she wondered if she might have gone to dinner with him under different circumstances. She shook herself internally.

Stop that shit right now, Nicole! she told herself. *You're not here because he's pretty.*

She smiled back at him in a way that caused a subtle shift in the shape of his eyes. For even as they continued to smile, she saw him become a predator. It was exactly what she was hoping for. Because at that moment she knew that he had crossed over a mental line. He'd been standing on the side marked "Might Get Laid," and had been happy to be there. But he was now on the other, where his left foot held steady on "Gonna" while his right kept time with the band on "Happen." On cue. Like a marionette.

Nicole knew where Guillermo liked to drink in the afternoon, and she knew that his line of work, (although what that line was exactly she'd yet to discover, much to her chagrin), allowed him flexible hours, so that drinking in the afternoon was a regular thing. She even knew what time he liked to get started. Waiting until four p.m., when the Electric Lumberjack's happy hour officially commenced, was not good enough for Guillermo. He never stepped foot in the bar before 4:06, proving to himself, every day, that he was not an alcoholic. She'd heard him so much as say so to the bartender more than once.

The waiter came with their drinks and Nicole ordered. She got an appetizer sampler, joking that she'd share it with Guillermo. (He wasn't going to even get to look at it for long!) Then, to his obvious surprise, she ordered a Four-Alarm Burger as her entrée. She knew that the appearance she'd adopted for the day would have led him to expect her to order something a little more sophisticated, and pricey.

She smiled at him as the waiter left, and heated that to four-alarm status as well. She knew that if she'd been hugging him now, things would feel a little different. She actually felt a twinge of disappointment. She had expected a little more from him. He was putty. He was a puppy.

He was a putty puppy.

A sound distracted Nicole. She shifted her eyes and what she saw caused her to narrow them slightly. A group of businessmen were being seated at the only table between her and the front door. If she was being honest, it wasn't *that* big of a deal. There was only one seat that blocked her view of the portal, and that was only for the instant that it opened. As soon as the person stepped inside she could pick them up. It was just an annoyance. Things had been going so well, and now there was a fly on the people-side of the screen-porch.

She began to return her attention to Guillermo, but her eyes snapped back to the head blocking the door. He looked nothing like the man with whom she was dining. His face was not sculpted in the way Guillermo's was. His hair was not glued in place, and it was cut in a way that it seemed to fall as it wished, but still managed to look perfect. And...was that a trace of gray by the temples?

Now Nicole forced herself to focus upon Guillermo. He had nearly finished his drink, a double bourbon on the rocks, and was holding his glass aloft to catch the waiter's eye. She frowned slightly, thinking once more how absurdly easy this cleaning was going to be. But she made her face soften again before he looked back. When he did, Nicole saw that he was still fully enamored and fully convinced his dreams were soon coming true.

So she stole a glance at the anti-Guillermo again. Then with a trained sweep that looked like nothing more than a casual glance to any observer, she sized up the men that accompanied him. The corners of her lips may have dipped a little as she saw they were dweebs. They were obviously hoping to strike a deal with Block-head—*that's* two *nicknames for a man I've been aware of for exactly twenty seconds,* she thought—and they obviously think they're a whole hell of a lot slicker than him. *Just like Darlene always says: "Slicker than pig-shit."*

"Bethany, is everything alright?"

Nicole was actually startled at the sound of Guillermo's voice. She'd intended only to steal a glance at the table, but had ended up staring at Mr. Bighead for nearly a minute—now three nicknames

"No, I'm fine," she said recovering quickly. "I was just looking for our waiter. I am freaking starving!" The answer seemed to amuse and satisfy Guillermo and she was glad. Because she wasn't kidding. She hadn't eaten all day and it was all she could think…

He was the only one at the table that was eating. The other two were jabbering on and on, talking turns sounding like obvious assholes, but he just nodded from time to time as he kept shoveling in… what? Fajitas—*Oh, my God, those smell amazing!* She giggled as a pepper dove from the shell onto his suit jacket. *His wife is going to be pissed,* she thought. Then, in an action that later caused Nicole to question if it had been some kind of evolutionary knee-jerk, she looked at his left hand. She grinned more obviously as she saw no ring. Then she gasped as she realized his clear brown eyes were gazing directly into hers. He was smiling slightly too. But immediately he looked away as one of the toads grabbed his forearm to drive home whatever insipid point he was making. She turned her attention begrudgingly back to Guillermo. His expression had cooled slightly.

Nicole quickly realized she was being careless. She was here to clean Guillermo, not to keep stealing glances at an obstruction —*with the cutest laugh I've ever heard.* It sounded genuine, despite the fact that it was in response to something one of the slugs was saying.

"Bethany! Do you want to reschedule our dinner? You seem… preoccupied." Guillermo almost looked angry now. No, not angry, Nicole realized. He looked hurt. The word "reschedule" echoed in her head like a voice did on summer nights on Lake Hartwell back home. Over and over.

"No!" she said, a little too forcefully. "No, no rescheduling!" His countenance brightened slightly seeing that she clearly did not want to lose him.

She was in fact thinking about the weeks of work she'd put in to make this night happen. There was no way in hell anything was getting rescheduled. Besides, there was the *other* thing that she hadn't really thought much about so far. Darlene had picked up some chatter that indicated there may be another admirer in the house that night. It was no more than a couple of snippets of heavy static with a few sentences tucked inside, but Darlene's gut told her there may be a second assassin at the Western, perhaps connected with Guillermo, or perhaps only using him as a fortuitous magnet. But in either case he was there to kill Nicole.

As she thought about it now, it was so like a black and white spy movie that it made her chuckle. She was here to kill Guillermo García, Spanish Nation, recent convert to Islam, recruited by Al Qaida, and at the vanguard of a buildup of radical sleeper cells in the U.S., poised for some big statement in the near future. The approaching millennium seemed like a logical time for an uptick in terrorist activity. The problem was that Guillermo was from a powerful family, and should he fall prey to anyone with connections to the government, it would cause a level of embarrassment that official channels could not tolerate.

So the job came to the Cleanup Crew. And because there was no one that Darlene, the Executive Direction of the CUC and the woman who'd recruited her, trusted more with such a potentially volatile situation, it was given to Nicole.

And somebody had been handed a file with her name on it as well. One of her names anyway. She never used the same one twice, and her "real" name was not circulated.

The scenario was delightful enough before the distraction. *The perfectly delightful distraction.*

"I need to excuse myself," Guillermo said, snapping her eyes back to him yet again. "I must visit the men's room."

As he stood, she could see that he was now coming very close to being angry. "I'll be waiting," she said, with all the musk she could infuse into three words. He didn't make it all the way back to happy at hearing it. Now he just looked confused.

When he left, she took one more look at anti-Guillermo, Blockhead, Mr. Bighead, and then stood herself. As much as she would have liked to find out this man's given name, so that she could stop using adolescent nick names, Nicole realized she'd been handed a gift.

The layout of the restaurant placed the restrooms completely out of sight from the dining room, with the men's and lady's rooms on opposite walls, facing one another. On the back wall of the narrow hallway, about six feet past the restrooms, was an emergency exit. It was the sort that sounded an alarm when opened, but Nicole had disabled that feature the day before. She would slip into the men's room, fire one suppressed round into the back of Guillermo's skull and be out the back door before his swarthy ass hit the floor.

The only problem, as she opened the door, was the Guillermo didn't appear to be in the lavatory. Smiling mischievously, she turned and opened the woman's room door. *That rascal!* she thought. But he wasn't in there either.

"Well, shit," she said aloud. She'd watched him turn the corner into the hallway. There were no other options. He had to have gone down this hallway. But if he wasn't in either bathroom he had to have gone...

"Outside," Nicole said, speaking aloud to herself again. *Is he trying to run out on me?* she wondered. No one ran out on Nicole Jacks! Especially not someone she was being paid to clean. Attempting to push it open silently she slipped into the dimly lit back alley. Before it could close Guillermo had his right arm around her from behind, and his left hand held a very lustful blade to her throat. Not the protrusion she'd hoped for during their second embrace.

"And so, you will not complete your mission tonight. You will not be the one to strike a blow. That honor is reserved this night for Allah. Do you think we do not know who you are, Katherine?"

There are many times in life when laughter is absolutely appropriate. Dozens of situations list "laughter" prominently in their list of suitable reactions. This was probably not one of them.

Yet that's exactly what Nicole did. She burst into boisterous laughter, to such a degree that Guillermo's blade actually passed across her skin slightly, opening a tiny cut. She didn't feel it.

Because at the exact same time she simultaneously lifted her right foot and drove her heel into his foot, right at the base of the shin, and she used her right thumb to flip open her purse. He released her immediately and as Guillermo's screams of pain filled the otherwise vacant alley, she pulled the 228, and spun around. He was hopping comically on his uninjured foot. She laughed again. "Katherine? That's the one you stupid fuckers settled on as my real name? I don't even remember what I used as a last name with that alias. Warren, maybe?"

"Watson," said Guillermo weakly as he continued to hop in pain, even as he raised his hands in recognition of the fact that he was still probably going to get fucked, just not in the way he'd been hoping.

"Katherine Watson! Yes! Very good, Guillermo. If only you were as good at choosing a philosophy of life. The one you picked gets you dead a lot."

Although he could not put weight on his bleeding foot, Guillermo stopped hopping and glared at Nicole. "You know nothing of what you speak. Allahu Akb…"

Nicole fired three shots, center mass, before he could finish. He crumpled to the ground as the nine millimeter holes in his chest recolored his white shirt a rich, dark red. When he completed his landing, Nicole stood over him and looked down. "Yep. God is greater. But you're a piece of shit." She knew he was probably already dead, but the moment seemed as though it needed a solid punchline. She reached into her purse, putting the gun away and extracting a small glassine envelope containing some low-grade heroin. She dropped it on the ground by his body. Nothing to see here. Just a drug deal gone wrong.

Nicole looked briefly at the closed back door of the Western Wine Bar. A sad smile spread across her face. "Goodbye, Blockhead," she said, deciding that was her favorite. "Oh, what might have been." She disappeared into the night.

ONE WEEK LATER, Nicole Jacks sat once again in the Western. She was not working. It was uncommon for her to revisit the scene of a job, but just as she'd hoped, when the body of the slain Spaniard was discovered, the smack was found as well and the police called it a sour drug deal.

So tonight was a celebration of a job well done. And a lucrative one at that, as Darlene had told Nicole her lifetime earnings as a cleaner had exceeded a million dollars. As she sipped champagne while waiting for her appetizer, she wondered what her old man would think of his June-bug being a millionaire.

Then thoughts of her father evaporated as Nicole could barely contain her excitement. For against all odds a man walked through the front door of the Western. The weather had begun to cool a week further into autumn and he handed a navy blue overcoat to the coat-check, but when he turned she saw that her first observation had been accurate. It was Blockhead.

As if his just being there wasn't enough to feel like she'd passed through a rain shower of good karma, he took the same seat at the same table as he had the week prior. And he was alone, although he appeared to be waiting for someone as he continued to alternate between looking over his shoulder and at his watch.

Nicole continued to sip at her wine and pretended to take no notice of him. If he was waiting for a business associate she might consider hanging around until the meeting ended. If he was waiting for a woman, she'd quietly slip away, and that would be that.

It soon became clear that neither of those outcomes were going to happen, because he was clearly being stiffed. She kicked around a few potential opening lines, and was just about to approach him when she saw him stand, his Manhattan in hand. *Damn,* she thought at first, *I waited too long. He's leaving.*

But he was *not* leaving. And instant later he stood next to her table. "Are you alone tonight?" She'd been in mid-sip and was forced to nod and offer a close-lipped "Mmm-hmm."

"Well it appears my meeting didn't show." *Good, it* was *business.* "I think my table is a little better than yours. You wouldn't consider joining me, would you?"

His table was decidedly *not* better than hers. Tactically it was a shit-show. But for the first time in many years, she didn't care. "God, I thought you'd never ask," she said, extending a slim and perfectly manicured hand. "Nicole Jacks," she said.

Dan took her hand. She saw him look at her opposite hand as he took her right. He was doing the same thing she'd done the prior week: scanning for a wedding ring. Not seeing one apparently encouraged him as he raised her hand to his lips and kissed it gently. "Dan Porter. Damn glad to meet you," he said.

She laughed in a way that, even to her own ears, sounded more genuine that any sound she'd made in a long time. She grabbed her clutch, another reward she'd given herself... a night out with no mom purse hiding her weapon, and her drink and moved to his table.

The meal was fantastic. Her Four-Alarm Burger tasted far better than she could have imagined, and Dan Porter turned out to be every bit as real, down to earth, and absolutely gorgeous as she first imagined he would be.

"I have a confession to make," Dan said.

"Oh, confessions already? Dish!"

"I never thought you'd say yes to dinner with me after the guy I saw you with last week."

Nicole smiled enigmatically. Apparently, Dan didn't follow

the news or hadn't connected the dead "drug dealer" with the man Nicole had joined for a meal. Almost offhandedly she said, "You don't have to worry about seeing him again."

Dan smiled broadly at that news. He lifted his drink, "In that case, here's to the beginning of a beautiful friendship."

She lifted her champagne flute and clinked it against his, "That's Bogart, right? Nice." She smiled broadly as well.

THE GREAT GAZOO

Carlton knew that 166st Street in the Bronx was not the safest place to be laid out in that exclusive parcel of real estate enjoyed so often by people of his station; the gutter. He looked up at the lights of the Ogden Avenue Rite Aid; his night light. He'd spent the better part of the day up and down 166th, asking those he passed if he might lighten the burden of pocket change under which they suffered. He'd not been completely unsuccessful. But the folks that lived in the apartment buildings around there hadn't selected them for their luxury appointments. No one had much in this neighborhood and what they did have they were disinclined to hand over to a fellow such as Carlton.

A wooden barrier fence, heavily covered in graffiti, stood just to the right of where he was laying. Beyond that was the dirty red awning of the Family Dollar. It didn't smell very nice in this gritty part of town, but neither, he had to admit, did he. Carlton reached into the pocket of his filthy mustard-colored suit jacket and extracted a narrow bottle. There were about five swallows left of the Mad Dog 20/20 that had been burning its way down his gullet since just after the dinner hour. Supper, which had consisted of a burrito found with a bite-mark indicating the need for some orthodontic work, screamed desperately to be washed down. He took three of the five swallows. "Ah, the Dog!" he said to himself, savoring the wine that has been described as being "as majestic as the cascading waters of a drainpipe."

As he flopped in the gutter no one even looked his way. It was easy to be invisible in the Bronx. Even the people who lived *inside* the buildings, as opposed to Carlton, who most definitely lived *outside,* were more or less anonymous. Kids played with other kids, but the adults mainly kept to themselves. And a guy like Carlton, well he was born to be stepped over. Or rolled, if he drank so much that he passed out on the street. Not that he had much to steal. His pockets were empty and no one was going to remove any of this clothing for their own use, unless they needed a rag to wipe bird art off their windshield. And his shoes had more holes than the story he told the cops when they came by to roust him: "Waiting for my daughter, officer. She's s'posed to pick me up after her PTO meeting."

But usually by the time the sort of people who stole from bums hit the streets, he'd moved into a nice cozy dumpster for the night. However, it was not time for bed yet. This was still the relaxin' hour.

Carlton's story was so cliché that he didn't even tell it to himself anymore. Lost job, lost house, lost wife, blah blah blah. Nobody cared, least of all Carlton. It was far too late, in his opinion, to continue to mourn all the things that were no longer a part of his life. Except perhaps his dignity. He checked his pants to make sure he hadn't wet himself. Nope. Dignity, Carlton told himself, was intact. As long as he could get his hands on something potent to drink by the afternoon, he was fine with it all.

He looked at the bottle. Two more swallows. Should he save them for later, or finish them now? It was while he was pondering this deep life-altering decision that something caught his attention. It had suddenly grown quiet. The Bronx was never quiet. Not at seven in the evening, or three in the morning. Always cars honking and tires screeching, always people shouting in Spanish, "Oye, 'mano! Háblame!" And always the girls at night, "Hey, handsome, do you want a date?" Never to Carlton, of course, but never far away from him either. All around him, always. Cities made noise and the borough that was home to the Yankees and Fordham University was no exception.

So, for it to have grown absolutely quiet was beyond odd. It was other-worldly. "That settles it," he said to himself as he tossed the dregs of the Mad Dog back. If this was the rapture, he wasn't going to be carried to the clouds with anything left in the bottle that they'd probably make him dump out at the gates. As he swallowed the last of it he let the container slip from his hand onto the pavement. There should have been a clink, maybe even a smash as the glass hit the asphalt. But there wasn't. "Jesus," thought Carlton. "What the hell." He looked to where the bottle should have landed. There it was, unbroken. And spinning. It was spinning in the street like it was waiting to point out the girl he was going to kiss. But there was no girl.

There were feet however. Two feet, maybe a size 10 ½, in some kind of flashy new kicks like the kids always wore. Like them, but unlike them at the same time. These were the snazziest he'd ever seen. *They can't afford food, but they find a way to get two-hundred dollar shoes,* he thought, perhaps overly judgmentally considering his own circumstance. He lifted his eyes to see the punk that was probably about to kick the snot out of him, so that he could give a good description to the police later.

Instead he saw a man with white hair. Snow-white hair, but a face that looked no more the twenty-five. Blue eyes that looked somehow wrong, and a shining green earring that dangled from his left lobe. His eyes jerked involuntarily back to that hair. It stood straight up, like Duke Nukem from the computer game when he was a kid, only taller. This hair was much, much taller. The man was staring at him, intently. Apparently, Carlton had lost his veil of invisibility.

"What do you want?" Carleton asked. He didn't bother asking "Who are you?" What difference would that have made? But it was the unasked question that the man answered.

"My name is Umlaut Five," he said.

"That's perhaps the most messed up name I've ever heard. What *is* that, German or something?"

"I have no nationality. But I'm not from here." He paused then added "Not from here, exactly." As if that cleared everything up.

Carlton looked now at his clothes. The man wore neatly-pressed khaki slacks with more pockets than one would believe could actually be fit onto two pant legs. Carlton started to count them, but then noticed the shirt. He supposed it was silver lamé or something like that, something the disco douchebags would have worn back in the Seventies. In college, he'd thrown food at guys who wore shirts like that. It looked an awful lot like aluminum foil, Carlton thought, but who the hell wore clothes made of Reynolds Wrap?

"Ok, so-called Mr. Five. I ask again: what the hell do you want?"

"I want to show you things, Carlton. Wonderful things."

Carlton shook his head unequivocally. "I'm not into that.

There's plenty of guys around who'd love to look at your 'wonderful things,' but I'd be much happier if you kept your crazy pants up." That was the last thing Carlton needed, to be hustled by some disco leftover.

"And how do you know my name?" he asked as an afterthought.

"I know all about you. Carlton Brewster, age forty-six, formerly employed on Wall Street by Goldman Sachs, formerly married to Evelyn Brewster née Feinstein. Born in Binghamton, New York, undergrad at Fordham – top of your class, MBA from NYU Stern – also top ranked. You should have had it all and were once on your way to getting it, but instead you have nothing. Down and out and alone on the streets of New York City, begging for enough money to get yourself drunk every night. Does that sound about right, Carlton?"

"So, you're a P.I. then. Who sent you to find me? Certainly not Ev. She doesn't want anything to do with me. Do I have some bastard kid somewhere that I don't know about? Tell your client I'm sorry, but I don't have any money to pay her child support."

"No I am not a private investigator, Carlton. Actually, I am a tailor by trade."

"That would explain all the damn pockets," Carlton said. "Practicing on your own pants?"

"The pockets. Yes. Quite."

Carlton looked at him again. *He certainly isn't going to have a lot of customers, making clothes like that,* he thought. Umlaut's face bothered him. He couldn't quite nail down why. Those eyes were definitely weird, (did the blue iris fill the entire eye?) but there was something else as well, something he was too drunk to readily identify.

"So, what does a tailor want to do with a street bum?" Carlton asked.

"As I told you, I have things to show you. Wonderful things."

"You keep saying that, and I keep telling you that I don't want to see your unit. I don't care how much you want to pay me."

"I have no intention of showing you my genitalia, Carlton. I couldn't if I wanted to. I do not have any."

That gave Carlton a start. No package? A war veteran then? Like Bill Hurt in *The Big Chill*, only from Afghanistan instead of Viet Nam probably.

Umlaut explained. "No one from my time has genitalia. There is no more sexual reproduction. We have found it to be a very ineffective way of creating new life. There are too many things that can go wrong. No, I am a synthetic human. Crafted, not born."

"Your *time* did you say?" This was not the sort of conversation one had on 166th Street in early June, on a pleasant evening at about eight p.m. "What time are you from? Nineteen Seventy-Eight, fresh from Studio 54 with that friggin' shirt on?"

"No, I'm not from the past, Carlton. People still had genitals in Nineteen Seventy-Eight."

"Not the disco boys. Listen, Umlaut, was it? I'm a drunk. I'm a bum. A 'street person' the liberal politicians like to say these days. I'm a wasted human being. But I'm not so far gone that I don't get what you seem to be implying. Are you trying to tell me that you're from the future?"

"Fifty Thousand years in the future to be precise."

Carlton started to stand up. He'd had just about enough of this malarkey. He'd been living on the streets for nearly eight years now, and had seen all manner of bad people. But this cat was clearly deranged to a degree that set off all sorts of tingling warning bells, and that meant he was probably dangerous. Maybe the sort of person that liked to slice the skin off your fingers nice and slow, just to listen to the music of your screams. He stumbled as he tried to get his feet under him. The man grabbed his arm and steadied him.

"Please, just leave me alone, Great Gazoo."

"Of course. 'The Flintstones,' 1961 to 1966. The Great Gazoo was voiced by the renowned comic actor Harvey Korman, who rose to considerable fame on the 'Carol Burnett Show,' 1967 to 1978. Ancient animated entertainment is one of my hobbies, Carlton. Thank you for making that reference. There are of course errors in your allusion, however. The Great Gazoo was an alien. I am not. He was about two feet tall, and he levitated. I cannot levitate, and I am six foot three and one half inches tall. He also had a disproportionately large head. My head is well suited to my body. And finally, if I *were* the Great Gazoo, I would be referring to you as 'Dum-Dum,' and not by your given name."

"Yes. I remember the cartoons, too."

"Of course, you had the privilege of watching them when they were new. I have only seen them in the archive of ancient history. Fortunately, many have been well preserved. Others have been lost, sadly, and only trace records remain. For example, it is said that Pebbles and Bam Bam later had their own show. I should have liked to have seen it."

"You didn't miss much there," Carlton said, "Except for maybe Schleprock."

"A synthesis of Yiddish and pseudo stone age! Delightful!"

"Yeah, he was a barrel of laughs. Listen. What going on really? Is this some hidden camera show? Because I'm not going to sign the release unless you guys come across with some green. No one makes a buck off Carlton Brewster unless he gets a taste."

"There are no hidden cameras, Carlton, although my sponsors can see everything that we are doing, and can hear everything we're saying."

"Your sponsors? Then you're from AA. I'm not interested, twelve-step."

"No, Carlton. I'm not from Alcoholics Anonymous. That organization is no longer needed in my time. We have cured addiction. That is not the reason I've come to you. I do not wish to sit in judgment of your habits. I wish to show you..."

"Wonderful things. Yeah. You told me." Carlton was pretty drunk, but not enough to explain all of this. Only insanity could explain this. Either his own, or Umlaut Five's. Someone was crazy. That was clear.

"I suppose I shall have to show you something wonderful in order for you to believe me. Your mind is just too closed off to reality for you to take my word for anything."

"Reality. What a concept."

"Perfect. Robin Williams. Nineteen seventy-nine. A vinyl record album. He was a genius. We mourn his early passing to this day."

"To this day? He's only been dead for two years."

"Fifty thousand and two. You're going to have to adjust your frame of reference." As Umlaut spoke, Carlton was shocked to see that Robin Williams was now standing beside him.

"Where did you come from?" Carlton managed to sputter.

"Mommy always said I came from heaven," Robin Williams replied. It certainly seemed to be him, alright. Carlton was at a loss. Still convinced that this was all some kind of elaborate hoax, he was none the less unable to think of anything to say in response to this new development. Nor could he offer any rational explanation. Except for a sudden onset brain tumor, maybe.

"The first of the wonderful things," said Umlaut. "Robin Williams himself, here to greet you."

"Nanoo," said Robin Williams.

"How ... who ... what in the hell?"

As the three of them stood in the gutter of the abandoned Bronx street, (for as far as Carlton could see in any direction, there was no one else), Umlaut Five placed his hand on Carlton's shoulder, speaking soothingly. "I recognize that seeing Robin Williams must be unsettling. He has been dead for fifty-thousand years, after all."

"Fifty-thousand and two," Robin Williams corrected.

"And two. Yes. But you see Carlton, in the era from which I come to you, we have been able to resurrect, for lack of a better term, many great people from human history. Of course, that includes many thousand years of history which to you has not yet come to pass."

Carlton just looked at him, his mouth slightly open.

"You made that fortuitous reference to Robin's famous record album, so I selected him to show you. Had you mentioned John Lennon, for example, I could have brought him. Or Caesar, or Oscar Wilde, or Justin Bieber."

"You're kidding. You resurrected Justin Bieber? He's not even dead yet. And he's an ass-wipe."

"Justin Bieber has been dead for fifty-thousand years and one day."

Carlton tried to wrap his misty mind around the mathematics couched in that statement. "So, um, he's going to die tomorrow?"

Umlaut Five cast his eyes down. "Sadly, yes."

"That's actually the first *good* news you've given me. I'd ask you why you chose to bring him back at all, but I don't think I'm ready for the answer to that one."

Robin Williams laughed. Carlton looked at him. "Hey, I was just as surprised as you are," he said. "For some reason the sexless girls of Tomorrow Land still dig him. I don't get it either."

Umlaut addressed them both. "The things we value in my era diverge greatly from what mattered to you in yours. Still, there are many great heroes of the past upon which we can agree. Pee Wee Herman, for example."

Carlton again stared at the white-haired man.

"No, no. Pee Wee's totally legit," said Robin Williams in response to Carlton's blank expression. "Not like Bieber."

"We've much more to discuss than just the people whose essence we have preserved," said Umlaut Five. "We should walk."

Carlton looked to the ground and saw that his empty Mad Dog bottle was still spinning like a propeller. He pointed to it. "Are you doing that?"

Umlaut Five looked down, noticing the phenomenon for the first time. "Hmm. It's probably my shoes," he said, offering no further explanation. Carlton took another look at the tricked-out sneakers and then nodded his head. *Fair enough,* he thought. He was unprepared to pursue the topic any further.

The white-haired man began to walk toward Martin Luther King Boulevard. Robin Williams fell in behind him, and turned to look back at Carlton. He waved for him to follow them. Reluctantly, Carton did.

As they moved along the street, Carlton saw that the stillness followed them. Past MLK Boulevard, Carlton could see the Deegan Expressway. It was abandoned. "What happened to everyone else?"

sn't quite following. "Everyone else? Who do you
I can show them to you."

g about the million and a half people who call the
sweet home. Everyone except for the three of us
vanished."

Uh, . _ :. They've not gone anywhere. They simply cannot
see us now, and you cannot see them. It is a byproduct of the
Quantum Inertial Field, QIF for short."

"Oooo," said Carlton. "That sounds science-y."

"You turn an interesting phrase, Carlton. Yes, it falls within
the realm of applied science. In your time, it would have been
assigned to theoretical physics most likely. But in my era, it is
generated by an inexpensive device with very few moving parts. I
got mine at Best Buy."

"There are still Best Buy's in the future?"

"Yes. Same off-kilter yellow tag and everything. Although now
instead of laptop computers and DVD's they sell Inertial Field
generators. And cappuccino makers. Those are a hot item."

"They still have KFC, too," said Robin Williams. "I've been. I
can't put my finger on it, but it's not as good as I remember it."

"Perhaps only ten of the eleven herbs and spices made it
through to the future. Maybe one went extinct," Carlton offered.

"I do not know about the recipe," said Umlaut Five, "but I can
tell you that the chickens are painstakingly manufactured in
some of the cleanest factories you have ever seen."

Robin Williams put his hand to his mouth, as if to stop
himself from throwing up. "You never told me that," he said to
Umlaut Five.

"You didn't ask. And if I remember correctly you ate seven
pieces. It didn't seem to bother you at the time."

"That was before I knew they came from factories and not from eggs."

"It probably wasn't much different in our time, pink slime and all that," Carlton said to the comedian. "Let's face it, the whole meat industry is pretty sketchy. Or was pretty sketchy. Mr. Five, I'm confused. Have we traveled to your time? Is that why I can't see anyone but you two?"

"Goodness, no!" Umlaut Five replied. "This neighborhood will look completely different in fifty-thousand years."

"How so?" asked Carlton, beginning to forget his initial skepticism, much to his own surprise.

"Well, first of all, a good deal of it would be under water."

"Say what, now?"

"Unfortunately, much of the damage done to the environment by the careless people in your era, and those who lived in the two hundred-fifty growingly industrialized years or so prior to your birth, could not be reversed. Greenhouse gasses raised the temperature of the Earth sufficiently for the polar ice caps to melt. This occurred within only a century from your era, give or take. Much of both coasts of what you called North America, and indeed all of the continents, found themselves submerged by the rising ocean waters."

"So Al Gore was right."

"Albert Arnold Gore, 45th vice president of the United States," said Umlaut Five. "A true visionary and a great ruler, becoming the First Director of the Global Human Collective."

"Say what, now?"

"Within your lifetime, Carlton, the concept of individual nations will be abolished. This is something you should be quite proud of."

"Why me?"

"Because you will play a pivotal role in the establishment of the GHC."

"Global Human Collective?"

"Exactly. Perhaps I should let Mahatma Gandhi explain."

And just like that, Gandhi, dressed in his famous beggar's robes and round-framed glasses, joined the party.

"I'm not sure I am the best person to explain the GHC," Gandhi said to Umlaut Five. "I was concerned primarily with the former nation of India, and with non-violent disobedience."

"Yes, but in my era you hold an important position in the Collective."

"He does?" asked Carlton, as he reached to shake Gandhi's hand.

"Yes. He plays the bass guitar in the GHC orchestra."

Carlton lifted his left eyebrow. He lifted it like a boss... like Spock... and Umlaut Five was very impressed. "Eyebrow lifting is a lost art," he said. "We no longer have the facial muscles required to execute that particular maneuver."

That was what was wrong with his face, Carlton realized! The musculature was all wrong. Heavy cheek development, but not much in the way of anything above the jawline. Oddly it made his face look more primitive that it did evolved.

"Still, I know the significance. You are mistrustful regarding what I've said."

"Well, yeah!" said Carlton, a little loudly. "I mean for the most part playing bass isn't even a significant role in a garage band, let alone in a global government."

"Don't forget about Jaco Pastorius," Gandhi said, a little miffed at Carlton.

"That would be different. If he had told me that Jaco was the bass player for the world-wide orchestra, I'd have been a little more impressed. No offense."

"Hmph," said Gandhi.

"Oh, I'm afraid you've hurt his feelings," Umlaut Five said. "Gandhi is quite an amazing bassist. He plays fretless, just like Jaco."

Carlton was getting more lost as the conversation went on. "At least tell me you brought Jaco back."

"Oh, most definitely. He is happily employed in a KFC chicken factory."

"Oh come on!" said Carlton, very loudly. "The more you tell me, the more all of this sounds like bullshit. I was almost willing to play along for a minute there, but you're telling me that the greatest bass player who ever lived now manufactures artificial chickens, while one of the greatest peacemakers ever to walk the planet is jamming on a fretless Fender? And that makes him a significant member of the global community?"

"I'll admit that the conversation has gotten a little muddled. Perhaps Justin Bieber could explain it better."

"You bring him here and I will kick you right in your Ken doll crotch."

"Really, Umlaut," said Robin Williams. "Hasn't Carlton suffered enough already?"

"Oh, alright. How about Kurt Vonnegut? Do you have any objections to him?"

"No, I love Vonnegut. But wait. Don't tell me that in your era he's a Toyota mechanic or something like that."

"Of course not. The automotive industry did not survive even your era, thanks largely to your work," Umlaut Five said. "No, Kurt Vonnegut is a writer in my era."

"Finally. Something that sounds rational."

"Yes. He writes cookbooks."

"I should have known," said Carlton. Still, he was quite pleased when Vonnegut appeared. "Hello, Mr. Vonnegut. I am a big fan of your work."

"Thank you. If you have a copy of *Great Desserts of the Southern Hemisphere* I'd be happy to sign it for you," Kurt Vonnegut said.

"Um, I was referring to the work you did while you were alive."

"Oh, that rot? Disregard all of it. Hi-ho."

"But you wrote some of the most significant books of the Twentieth Century."

"Mere bagatelles," Kurt Vonnegut countered.

"Please explain the Global Human Collective to Carlton, if you would," said Umlaut Five.

The four of them had climbed over the guardrail and were now leisurely walking across the Major William Francis Deegan Expressway. All six lanes of it. Carlton instinctively looked both ways, but there wasn't so much as a speeding tricycle to threaten his safety.

"You see, Carlton," said Kurt Vonnegut, "In a few years from the day we chose to visit you, the global economy will collapse. Too much debt and speculation, not enough oil and natural gas. The era of a petroleum based economy will be over. Despite that bad pork chop around the planet's neck being gone, greed and corruption will prevent the widespread use of renewable resources for quite some time. War will be rampant, as people fight over what little food and clean water remain. The Earth will grow dark, as will the hearts of man."

"Pretty depressing," Carlton said, not at all liking the narrative this iteration of Kurt Vonnegut was spinning.

"Indeed," he went on. "But then a pamphlet, a simple five-page folio, called 'Wake Up, for Chrissakes,' was published and it became a world-wide phenomenon. The author of the slim volume was a man named Carlton Brewster."

"Me," said Carlton. It was not a question. There was no incredulity in his tone. He said it flatly, without emotion. Yet in his head, fireworks were going off. *These people really are nuts*, he thought. He again scanned the Expressway, hoping just one car might come by that he could flag down to get him away from these maniacs. Nothing.

"Yes, most definitely you. In those five pages, you managed to outline a plan for world economic recovery, the end of international strife, and the need for a Global Human Collective, as well as a Global Human Collective orchestra."

"I mentioned the orchestra." Again, not a question.

"Yes. You realized, correctly, that music was a key element in universal understanding. I have you to thank for my resurgent popularity," said Gandhi. "Not that you seem to care." He was still miffed.

"Look, I'm sure you're an absolutely bitchin' bass player," Carlton said, trying to mend fences. Gandhi looked away, but gave just the slightest trace of a smile as Kurt Vonnegut went on.

"Although you clearly outlined everything that needed to be done, as well as explaining *how* it could be done, you had no interest in doing it yourself. That's where Al Gore came in. He traveled the world expounding the principles introduced in your pamphlet, and eventually garnered enough support for the GHC to rise out of the ashes of the doomed political landscape of the past." He turned to address the white-haired man. "Wouldn't you say the old way had become something of a slaughterhouse, Five?"

"Ah, I see what you did there," Carlton exclaimed, pointing to the cookbook author. Kurt Vonnegut gave an abashed little smile. "If you really considered all your pre-cookbook work to be rubbish, you wouldn't have uncorked that awful pun."

"You got me," said Vonnegut. "And so it goes."

"At any rate," said a voice with a heavy French accent from behind Carlton, "it was zee beginning of a global renaissance which continues to the present."

Carlton turned to see Napoleon Bonaparte struggling to keep up with the rest of them, his hand tucked in his shirt, his short legs pumping like pistons.

"I wouldn't think world peace would be your cup of tea," Carlton said to him.

"Well, I have zeen zee error of my ways, shall we zay," Napoleon Bonaparte replied. "Far better to conquer hunger, disease, poverty and death itself, than to conquer Russia. That is how I zee things now."

"Napoleon is a cracker jack fashion designer," said Umlaut Five, pointing to his shirt. "He introduced his aluminum foil line last year. Now everybody's wearing it."

"So it *is* Reynolds Wrap. Alright. Ok. Fine. Let's just say all of this is not the bad side effects of eating that partial burrito I found in the alley earlier," said Carlton. "Explain to me about the resurrection thing."

"Allow me to clarify," said Johnny Carson, who was now walking directly beside Carlton.

"Too bad Ed wasn't here to call you on," Carlton said.

"Ed doesn't do that anymore. There are no sidekicks in the future," Johnny Carson explained. "He's in hydroponic soybean production now. It's weird! But I digress. The resurrection of important figures from the past was first achieved around ten thousand years after your death, Carlton. A scientist – slash – modern dance instructor named Umlaut Two…"

"Any relation?" Carlton asked Umlaut Five.

"None whatsoever," he answered.

"Go figure," said Carlton.

"Umlaut Two was experimenting with micro-electric disturbances while between recitals, and his equipment was able to pick up the continued existence of what he called 'Permanent Life Essence.' In the less informed jargon of our era we called this 'the soul.' Umlaut Two found that archaic expression too laden with emotion, both good and bad, and opted for PLE instead."

"So, who did he come across?" Carlton asked.

"Justin Bieber," Johnny Carson said.

"Oh for the love of…"

"No, seriously. It just happened to be Bieber. Weird. What are the odds?" Johnny Carson asked, rhetorically.

"Approximate twenty-six point nine billion to one," said Leonard Nimoy, fully decked out in his Spock costume, complete with pointy ears, and walking between Gandhi and Robin Williams.

"He still gets a kick out of doing that," Johnny Carson explained.

"But my real passion is Putt-Putt golf," Leonard Nimoy explained.

"He won the Putt-Putt World Series three years running," Johnny Carson elaborated, reaching over to give him a playful punch on the arm. Apparently, he and Nimoy were good friends.

"I think you and Nimoy should have an eyebrow raising contest," said Robin Williams. "Umlaut would love that!"

By now they'd climbed down off the Deegan and were nearing the Harlem River. Like the empty streets, the dirty river was devoid of any indication that New York City was a populated location.

Carson continued. "The first attempts at actually physically resurrecting historical personages were not extremely successful. Mankind had not yet abandoned sexual reproduction and procreation was still the only method for creating a human body. Umlaut Two experimented with infusing the PLE into the body of a new born baby, but he knew even as he did so that the method was far from ideal, if for no other reason than the length of time it would take to determine of the child had developed the personality of the historical figure. It took almost five years for him to discover that his very first attempt had in fact worked – to some extent."

"To some extent?" Carlton asked the former late-night TV icon.

"Yes. That first infused child developed a severe case of dissociative personality disorder. One of the identities turned out to be a very disturbed psychopath. The other was Justin Bieber."

"Two sides of the same coin, in my opinion," said Carlton.

Genghis Kahn took up the story, as he moved to the front of the group. "It took another three centuries before scientists developed the method for completely synthesizing a human form. By then Umlaut Two had turned his attention almost exclusively to dance, but others had taken up his work in PLE infusion. With the advent of synthetic life, the process of infusion became much more successful, since the synths, as they were called, did not have a personality of their own."

"Or genitals of their own," added Robin Williams.

"Your English is quite good, Mighty Kahn," Carlton said. The Mongol emperor, now a lilac bush farmer, Carlton later learned, seemed flattered by the compliment.

"Thank you. I've had several thousand years to work on it. Napoleon had not tried as hard, I think."

The little Frenchman shrugged his shoulders. "Zee ladies love zee accent."

"Ooookay," said Carlton.

Genghis Kahn continued. "At any rate, the combination of synthetic life and PLE capture and infusion meant that persons from throughout the history of Planet Earth could now be 'resurrected,' although you can see now how that term does not quite work. The original bodies of these persons had long since decomposed, so in that sense they weren't really being resurrected. It was more like running a really snazzy program in a really high-end computer."

"Eventually," said John F. Kennedy, the latest to join the party, "the process of producing synths became so refined that scientists and later, after the work became commonplace, minimally trained technicians, could recreate the likeness of the historical figures down to the right colored shoelaces. It permitted me to make a great comeback."

"Did you assume a prominent political role in the GHC?" Carlton asked Kennedy.

"Actually, it allowed me to find a very fulfilling career in the manufacture of lace doilies. Sales are phenomenal," the former president said.

For several minutes, no one said anything. By now the group had swelled to about fifteen, as Henry Ford and Benny Hill appeared, along with both Olson twins and Bob Saget, together again. They stood on the right bank of the Harlem River, as a cool evening breeze ruffled all of their hair, with the exception of Umlaut Five, whose high-rise shock of white locks proved impervious to the wind. Carlton looked at each of the people that high school educated machinists were able, in that far distant vista, to bring to life. They all waited for him to react to all that they had told him.

"Frankly, I'm not sure I like the sound of this future. Apparently, life spans are greatly increased. Genghis spoke of Umlaut Two dancing well into his three-hundredth year. That part doesn't sound too bad."

"Death was the final disease to be cured," explained Socrates, his long gray hair moving slightly in the whisper of breeze coming off the river, "but it happened relatively quickly once they figured out the mechanics of it."

Carlton nodded to the great philosopher, who he was told now headed a carnival ring-toss game empire.

"But I guess I have a little problem with the whole synth thing. What happens if a couple just wants to have a baby? Not Harry Truman..." (Truman tipped his hat to Carlton), "or Clara Bow..." (the *It* Girl fluttered her eyelashes at him), "What if they just wanted little Umlaut Five, Jr.?"

Umlaut Five answered, "You simply call the factory and order one. I have two children, Sigh and Swallow."

"Sigh and Swallow Five?" Carlton asked.

"Precisely."

"What do they get for personalities if the synth isn't infused with someone famous?"

"Just a normal, perfectly adjusted life essence."

"Perfectly adjusted is not really normal, at least in my experience. But aside from that, I see a problem in the plot of this epic. Why would anybody pay attention to a five-page pamphlet written by a homeless alcoholic? I don't exactly inspire others to do great things, except maybe to stay in school so they don't end up like me."

"Your life is about to do a drastic about-face," Umlaut Five declared emphatically.

"Oh really," said Carlton. "And why is that?"

"Because of me," said a new voice. Carlton turned and saw the most beautiful five-year-old girl he'd ever laid eyes on. She was dressed in a delightful blue sundress, which matched the color of her crystalline eyes. An outrageous collection of blonde curls topped her head. Her smile instantly melted Carlton's heart. He then realized that he was almost completely sober, a state of being he avoided at all costs. He also realized he was completely at the mercy of this child.

"Who are you, little girl," Carlton asked her.

She put her small hands to her mouth and giggled. The laugh was the most beautiful sound that had ever reached his ears.

"I won't tell you who *I* am," she said playfully, "but I'll tell you who *you* are."

Carlton bent down to get close to her, as she indicated that she wanted to whisper into his ear. "You're my daddy," she said in her tiny voice, which was like a teacup full of sunshine.

Carlton straightened up quickly, uneasily. "How...who...what in the hell?"

"You already said that," said Robin Williams, placing his arm around Carlton's shoulder. "Here's the scoop Carlton. It's a little tricky, so follow along. As a result of our visiting with you tonight, you are going to stop drinking. Your reputation won't be easily repaired. You're not headed back to Wall Street, but you will take a menial job and work hard. You will meet a woman who will see the good in you. She will stand beside you and help you further crawl out of the urban wastewater sluice in which we found you."

Carlton again raised his eyebrow. "He means the gutter. He's being silly," his future-daughter said, again giggling, again warming his heart.

"But then the economic collapse will come. Despite believing this is no world in which to bring a child, Helene here will be born." Robin Williams pointed to the girl.

"Helene," said Carlton to the child. "That name suits you." She beamed a smile at him.

"It will be your love for her that will open *your* eyes, which will bring you the great epiphany which will lead you to write the all-important 'Open Your Eyes, For Chrissakes,' which, I might add, is a very cool title."

"Jealous!" said Kurt Vonnegut

"At first only a handful will be printed. By you. At the Kinko's on Court Street in Brooklyn. One will come to the attention of none other than Al Gore, and with more than a few 'I told you so's,' he really gets the ball rolling. The rest is history. Or should I say the future. Whatever."

Helene had reached up and taken Carlton's hand.

"There is one more wonderful thing I would like to show you," said Umlaut Five. As he felt the warmth of Helene's hand in his, Carlton didn't think anything else could be more wonderful than this. Umlaut Five reached into one of his many pockets and extracted a small device. To Carlton's eye it looked rather like an early webcam, the spherical kind that used to sit atop your CRT monitor, sans the UBS cord. "My Quantum Inertial Field generator," he explained, pointing to the Best Buy logo on the side of it. Umlaut Five fiddled with the device for a moment. Then he turned his back to the river and pointed to at the dirty Bronx neighborhood which Carlton had chosen only a few hours earlier as a place to drink his wine and ignore the world, just as it ignored him.

Carlton faced the direction Umlaut Five indicated. Where there should have been dingy tenements and rundown high rise apartments, Carlton saw a vast, watery landscape, dotted with oases of green, and punctuated by human dwellings that soared out of the water and into the sky, shining red in a sun that was setting behind him, staining what appeared to be white marble with its last rays of the evening. The cramped city had been transformed into a utopian paradise, equal parts urban planning and rural re-emergence, all despite the vast span of swollen ocean.

"That is how the Bronx will look in fifty-thousand years. Thanks to you and the forward-thinking people who took up the challenge you set before them. You will not live to see it happen, but you will be one of the first people brought back when PLE infusion is perfected," Umlaut Five said quietly. "Helene will follow close after you. You will be with her for a very long time."

This was overwhelming beyond the scope of Carlton's ability to process. He gaped at the beautiful landscape, then turned his eyes again to the little angel whose tiny hand was safely wrapped in his. Finally, he turned to Umlaut Five. "This is amazing," was all he could manage to say.

"You have only yourself to thank," the man from the future said. The other synths nodded in agreement.

"So what happens now?" he asked.

"Hey you, by the river. Get the hell away from there!"

Carlton was started by the sound of an amplified voice and he looked toward the Deegan Expressway to see a police officer standing beside his patrol car, speaking through the vehicle's loudspeakers, as cars sped by in both directions.

He looked around and saw that all of his famous new friends were gone. So were Umlaut Five and Helene. He was alone, standing too close to the Harlem River, being yelled at by a very aggravated cop.

With a sudden sadness that he thought might crush him, he walked toward the policeman. It wasn't all the acclaimed people that he missed as he approached the guardrail. It was the little girl, whose warm touch he could still feel. If nothing else they had told him was true, he wanted Helene to be real. The joy that had leapt up inside of him when she'd reached for his hand was the first inkling of good that he had felt in years.

That and the knowledge that Justin Bieber would die tomorrow.

"You look pretty rough, buddy," the cop said as Carlton came alongside him. "Anyway, you can't be down there. That's private property, and in your condition, you might fall in."

"Actually, I'm feeling quite well. Very steady," Carlton said. "But I understand. I'll leave."

The cop looked closely at him. "Hey look, get in the backseat. I'm not supposed to, but I'll give you a lift to a shelter. You may still be able to get a bed tonight."

"You know what I could really use? A job," he heard himself saying, not quite believing his own words. "You don't know anybody that could use reliable help, do you?"

The officer looked at him, a little skeptically. "Whaddaya do?" he asked.

"Anything," Carlton answered.

"You know, what? I may have a lead. It's night shift. Nothing glamorous. Hard work. But I might be able to get you in right away. You can't go looking like that, though," he said, indicating Carlton's dirty, ragged clothes and distinctive aroma.

Just then Carlton's toe caught on something, and he almost tripped. He looked down to see a pair freshly washed and neatly pressed khaki pants, with a few extra pockets, as well as a denim work shirt. He bent down and picked them up. Looking at the tags he saw that they were just his size. "Maybe you could take me to the Y first? I'll grab a quick shower and change into these," he said holding up the clothing.

"Yeah, I guess so. But you gotta hurry. My buddy might find someone else to fill the job, and I can't be running you around all night."

"Sure, of course. I really appreciate this, Officer…"

"Williams," said the cop. "Robin Williams. You know, like the comedian. My dad was a big Mork and Mindy fan. You know, 'Nanoo.'"

"Yeah. I know. Thanks, Officer Williams," said Carlton, grinning like an idiot. "Thanks a lot."

"Lucky, you finding them clothes," he said as he held open the car's door.

Carlton climbed into the uncomfortable backseat and Officer Robin Williams got in and put the car in drive. As he pulled away, Carlton looked again at the clothes he'd found. In the pocket of the shirt he saw a small card. He pulled it out and flipped it over. In a crisp hand were written the words, "Best of Luck. See you in 50,000 years, Dum-Dum. Your friend, U5 (aka The Great Gazoo.)"

As they passed the corner of Ogden Avenue and 166th, a glint in the street caught Carlton's eye. He turned and saw an empty bottle of Mad Dog 20/20, still spinning madly. As the cruiser drove by it, the bottle abruptly stopped spinning and hit the street, smashing into a thousand pieces.

Carlton smiled, and thought that for him, the pieces might actually be coming together.

THE HUNTERS

Steve and Hippo had been friends since the third grade. In the tumultuous year of 1968, Steve Mills moved to the small town of Beacon Falls, and had quickly learned what it felt like to be an outsider. Even at the age of eight children can be inhumanly cruel, and a new kid was an easy target. For the first week of school, Steve, who at that age was a little smaller than most of the other boys, was picked on relentlessly. "New kid, shrimp, pee-wee, midget." Steve heard it all.

Jim Parker knew a little about being picked on. He'd been born in Beacon Falls, and was never targeted for being new or small. In fact, quite the opposite was true. Jim had always been bigger than the other kids, taller on his first day of kindergarten by about two inches than the next biggest, and stocky but not fat. It didn't matter that he wasn't obese. Just being bigger was enough for him to have earned the nickname Hippo. Over time he'd learned that it was easier to accept the moniker than to fight it, and it was by far better than the handle they'd given to Missy Cosgrove, who'd had the misfortune of not making it to the girl's room that time in first grade, becoming

"Pissy" Missy forevermore.

Hippo had watched how Steve handled himself that dreadful first week, gradually realizing that the kid seemed okay. Despite the constant provocation, he kept his cool, trying his best to avoid the antagonists rather than confront them. On Monday of the second week of school, when Steve was once again sitting by himself in the lunchroom, Hippo stood over him and asked, "Red Sox or Yankees?"

"Ew. Yankees, of course."

"Of course," Hippo had replied, smiling and setting his tray next to Steve's. From that day forward the two were inseparable. And even though Hippo wasn't the most popular kid in the third grade, his acceptance of Steve had been enough to cause the new kid hazing to die down. By the end of September, Steve Mills no longer felt like an outsider.

From very early on the boys found they had many common interests besides just their choice of baseball teams. They both loved Saturday morning cartoons, but not the sissy ones. They both loved rock and roll music, but not any of the guys that the girls thought were dreamy, except the Beatles who they both agreed were great despite all the screaming chicks. And they loved to hunt, which in a rural town like Beacon Falls was a rite of passage.

They made their first foray in the winter of 1970, when they were in fifth grade, and when both had begged for, and received, BB guns for Christmas. The $8.95 both sets of parents had shelled out for the matching Daisy Red Ryders turned out to be money well spent, as it kept the boys in the woods and out from underfoot all winter long.

That first day, though, had been a few miles shy of momentous. They spent every one of the nine daylight hours in the trees west of Pine Rock Road, most of the time without seeing a single thing at which to shoot. They really didn't know anything about how to stalk game at that point, making enough noise to scare away critters in the woods near the town of Seymour, five miles to the south.

So, most of the day they spent talking and laughing, as only ten-year-old boys can. They first lamented the fate of their beloved Yankees, who, two years post-Mickey Mantle, had finished a dismal fifteen games behind Baltimore. "Let's face it, we sucked!" said Steve as he poured a few BB's from the milk-carton type container into his Daisy.

"The only guy worth a shit is that rookie catcher, Munson." Hipp agreed.

"What the hell kind of name is 'Thurman' anyway?" Steve asked, shaking his head.

"It's better than Hippo," Hipp said. They both had a laugh about that.

"Don't forget about Hippo Vaughn," Steve said after the chuckles died down. "He was a hell of a pitcher, my gramps tells me. He was a Yankee for a few years."

"He was a Highlander," Hipp corrected. "They weren't the Yankees until 1913 and by then Hippo was a Cub, may God forgive him."

"Oh, excuse me, Mr. Baseball Encyclopedia." That brought another round of laughs.

After that they moved on to other topics. Hippo went on for a while about a new British band that he really liked called Black Sabbath.

"I don't know about them Hipp. They sing about the devil and shit."

Hippo was having none of it. "Listen, they got a song about Iron Man! No one else has a song about Iron Man. They kick ass and that's that. And besides the Stones sing about the devil and you like them."

"I think Mick Jagger *is* the devil," Steve admitted.

"There ya go. So don't be a pussy."

But ultimately, as it usually did, the topic came around to girls. Neither of them had the slightest idea what they'd do with one if a girl had actually liked them, but both had started to notice the young ladies.

"Missy Cosgrove's getting boobs," Steve said, his voice lowered as if the forest itself might blab.

"Pissy Missy? Come on, dude!"

"Hey, she never pissed her pants since I've known her. And besides, boobs are boobs, bruddah."

"Ha! So what are you gonna do with Pissy Missy's boobs?"

"Give 'em a good squeezin', I guess."

"You're a pervert."

"You'd do it. You'd squeeze the shit outta them tit-tays."

"Eww! She's got shit in her boobs? No thank you!"

That brought the most raucous round of laughter yet, and any animals they hadn't already scared away were long gone now.

But just before the sun went down, as the two boys sat side by side in the snow at the base of a tall White Pine, they heard a tell-tale rapping and Hippo spotted a downy woodpecker on a high branch of a bare Red Maple about thirty yards away. He pointed and Steve lined up a shot. The gun made its quiet popping sound, but it didn't disturb the bird. Neither did Steve's BB. As near as they could tell he not only missed the woodpecker, he missed the entire tree.

So Hippo gave it a try. He aimed the gun, squeezed the trigger and as the boys watched, the bird fell from the branch and landed at the base of the big Maple. They ran to find it and discovered that Hipp had shot the bird directly through the eyes, killing it instantly.

"Jesus, you're a crack-shot, Hipp!" Steve said, slapping his friend on the back.

Hippo looked at the bird as it lay in the snow. "Who knew?" he said.

When they were old enough for their parents to allow them to purchase their own .22 rifles, which they saved for by starting their own two-man lawn-mowing company, Steve and Hippo continued hunting together; squirrels at first, then rabbits. And when their dads were confident they could handle it, they'd let them take the hunter's safety course and had taken them deer hunting.

After that first year, 1974, when they were on the verge of leaving Long River Middle School behind they took their rifles out alone, both father's satisfied that they didn't pose a threat to anyone.

By the time they were in high school, no one remembered that Steve Mills had once been an outsider. Puberty had been kind to him. As they embarked upon their senior year Steve stood six feet tall and weighed one hundred eighty muscular pounds, with marquee good looks to go with the athletic body. He was the starting quarterback for Woodland Regional High School, and

easily the most popular guy in his class. There wasn't a girl who
didn't dream of walking the halls holding his hand. A lot of hearts
were broken when he'd started dating none other than Pissy
Missy, whose nascent fifth-grade boobs had blossomed into the
real thing. Her long auburn hair and brilliant blue eyes were
perfectly matched by her curvaceous body. Whenever the Woodland Hawks played, Missy was cheering in her short skirt,
shaking more than just her pom-poms.

Hippo had not fared as well. He'd continued to be bigger than
his classmates, weighing fully two hundred fifty pounds at age
seventeen. Though he actually carried the weight well on his six-
five frame, and he used his size to the benefit of the Hawks,
playing a very solid center on the offensive line, his hips were just
too broad, his stomach a little too round.

Of course, that didn't bother Steve. Their friendship, at least
on the surface, had remained constant, even when most of the
other guys tried to convince him that he was far too cool to
continue hanging around with Hipp. Steve told them to knock
their shit off, pointing out as the football season progressed that
at least three games might have not have gone their way if it
hadn't been for Hippo's blocking at center, probably more. But
that didn't stop them. Steve Mills may have long ago stopped
being the new kid, but Jim Parker was still the Hippo.

And though Steve would never admit it, Hipp noticed that
things *were* a little different between them now. The other guys
held parties, which if discovered would have gotten them all
kicked off the team. Steve was always invited, though Hippo
never heard about them till after the fact. And the reality that
Steve went to every one of the legendary gatherings, typically
held in the same woods that Steve and Hippo hunted, in fact

beneath the very Maple tree from which Hippo had scored their first kill, well, that wasn't lost on Hipp.

It all came to a head on the night of Homecoming. The Hawk's schedule that year had been tough, with losses at home early in the season to Crosby and Naugatuck that had preceded a string of eight wins, the last three on the road. If they beat their arch-rival Seymour at home that night, they were headed for the States. No team from Woodland had ever made it to the State Championship tournament.

So, when Hippo uncharacteristically missed a key block, causing Steve to not only get sacked deep in the backfield, but actually fumble the ball, allowing Seymour to recover and return it for the game-winning score, not even Steve could stop what happened next.

Hippo should have known something was up right away. At the homecoming dance Tad Butler, co-captain of the team with Steve and arguably the second-most popular kid at WRHS, came up and shouted to him over the music, "Hey Hipp, don't feel like a schmuck or anything. Coulda happened to anybody. Look. We're having a party at the Maple tree after the dance. Why don't you grab some beers and meet us there."

In his dejected mood, this was music to Hippo's ears. It had been feeling like the worst night of his life, but now it seemed like it might turn out to be the best. So as the dance wound down, Hipp left and went to Beacon Beer and Beverage. He wasn't eighteen until April, but the girl who was working didn't even look up at him when he put the case of Bud on the counter and slid her a ten. He grabbed the beers and started to leave.

"Hey!" the girl called. Hipp figured he was busted, and turned to face her guiltily. "You always pay ten dollars for an eight-dollar case of beer? Take tour change, dipshit!" she finished, to his embarrassed relief.

Hipp drove a 1974 Datsun 710, neither fast nor sexy, but it got him where he needed to go and tonight it was taking him to his first drinking party. There was a dirt road that had been carved out for the hunters in '72, and that's where everybody parked when there was a get-together at the Maple Tree. It ran for about a mile and a half into the forested areas, but by the time Hipp arrived the cars were already lined up to within a couple hundred yards of the highway. Hipp calculated that every kid in Connecticut must have come to party. He grabbed the beer and hiked the half mile from the end of the dirt to where the legendary tree grew. Even before he reached the clearing he could hear the laughter. Someone had a boom box, and the music was cranking. It was the soundtrack from "Saturday Night Fever," all disco, which Hipp hated, but even still he almost had to pinch himself. He was finally going to a football party!

When he came into the clearing and his round face was lit by the bonfire that was brightly burning, everybody looked up and called out, "Hippo!" One of the guys from the team ran up and took the beer, while a couple of others led him to the circle of kids around the blaze and handed him a cold one.

Hipp and Steve had been taking beer into the woods with them when they went hunting for a couple of years now, but they usually could only smuggle a six pack from Steve's dad's garage fridge, so Hipp's drinking experience was not to the level that these revelers were used to. Tonight, the drink flowed freely, and he was soon far more drunk than he'd ever been. Steve sat with Missy on the other side of the fire. He hadn't talked to Hippo at all during the dance or the party, and Hipp figured he was a little miffed about the missed block. A shot at the States had meant more to Steve than anyone. There were college recruiters at the game, and they were there for him. But as he tossed back another beer, Hipp thought, *It'll pass. Steve will still get into a good school. One fumble can't erase a whole season.*

By one-thirty the party showed no signs of slowing, but Hippo was. He already knew that he was way too drunk to drive the Datsun home, though he probably would anyway. Just about the time he had made up his mind to leave, a group of his fellow linemen came to where he was sitting. At first they just sat too, putting their arms around his back. "Good old Hippo," one said.

That was the signal.

Five of the biggest guys grabbed Hipp's arms and legs. He didn't know what was happening because they call kept saying "Good old Hippo," over and over again. They picked him up by his limbs, not an easy task even for the whole line, and then dropped him on the ground next to the fire. Still holding him securely, they struggled to restrain him, for Hippo was pretty sure this wasn't fun anymore and he was fighting to get up. He couldn't.

Hippo looked frantically to the fire, where Steve and Missy were still sitting. Steve had a strange look on his face, halfway between regret and resignation. As Hippo watched, Missy stood and walked to where they were holding him. Now the chant changed.

"Pissy Missy! Pissy Missy!" they droned. As Hippo watched in horror Missy stood over him and pulled down her Vegas Gold cheerleader panties. Squatting slightly, she urinated directly on his face. The rest of the partiers howled with laughter, and as he frantically shook his head to remove as much of the mess as he could, he saw Steve, still sitting there. With the piss in his eyes he couldn't be sure, but it looked to Hippo like he was smiling.

Before he could be sure, the football players dragged him away from the fire, out of the clearing all the way to the footpath that they'd gradually worn between the end of the dirt road and the Maple Tree, where they finally dropped him in a heap. "Get the fuck out of here, you fat loser. We coulda been in the States." Tad Butler threw a length of rope at him. "Why don't you pick a good, strong branch and hang yourself? Fuck off and die." His teammates turned and walked away.

Once he was far enough away from the clearing that he knew no one could hear him, Hippo broke down. Stumbling toward his car, his body shook with the intensity of his sobbing. His eyes were burning and though the tears were slowly washing away the urine, when he reached his car and began to drive home he did so with great difficulty.

High school was long behind two hunters now. They were well on the backside of their forties and with the passing of their "glory days" their fortunes had reversed somewhat. Steve had, despite his infamous fumble, had earned a football scholarship to Penn State, but had blown out his knee in his first practice, ending both his sports career and his chance at earning a degree. He'd come home to Beacon Falls with a full-blown addiction to pain pills, and although he managed to hold onto a job at the lumber mill, the lion's share of his money was spent at Grogan's Bar, where Missy Cosgrove served him drinks, even after they married and later divorced.

Hippo had gone to Cornell, both on a partial academic scholarship, and by working his ass off all four years to cover the balance of his tuition. From there he'd gotten into Harvard Law, passed the bar exam, and after ten years at a big firm in Manhattan, eventually returned to Beacon Falls as well, opening his own quiet practice. He hadn't spoken to Steve since Homecoming at the Maple Tree, although he'd seen him often. In a town the size of BF it was impossible not to see everyone who lived there at some point or another. But he just couldn't bring himself to speak with his old comrade. Something had broken in him that night. And even for all his success, especially when held to the mirror of Steve's failures, he still carried a shattered place in his brain.

In the end it was Steve who had finally broken the ice. Hippo was alone in the office in late October. He was half-heartedly going over some briefs while watching TV. The Yankees were in the World Series again, against the Phillies. It was game two, top of the fifth, with the score tied one to one when he'd gotten the call. Steve, phoning from the police station. "Hipp, I need your help. They just got me for DUI, driving home from Grogan's. I didn't know who else to call."

"It's not your first," Hipp said coldly.

"I know. That's why I need you. They're probably not going to go easy on me this time. You're the best lawyer in BF. I might be looking a time, Hipp."

Hippo let out a long sigh. *So it looks like you're doing time, then, you bastard,* he thought. But into the phone he said, "Did they set bail?"

"Five grand."

"Jesus, Steve. I don't carry that kind of money around." He hesitated, considering telling Steve to go fuck himself for the hundredth time since he'd picked up the receiver. But he didn't.

"It'll take me a while. Hang tight."

The truth of the matter was that he *did* have five thousand dollars at his disposal. He actually kept nearly ten in his safe. For a town of just over six thousand people, a lot of them seemed to get in trouble, and he'd helped more than one make bail over the years.

He arrived at the station an hour later, having sat at his desk for most of that time looking at the stack of bills and remembering Steve's face in the fire light over twenty years before, and the rest in his car for a while, outside the station, recalling his own burning eyes.

He went to the desk sergeant, handed over the five large and took care of the paperwork. Ten minutes later they led Steve out. He was still cuffed from the arrest.

"For Christ sake, Bill," Hipp said to the cop who had a firm grasp on Steve's arm. "You can take the frigging cuffs off now I think. It's Steve Mills, not the Son of Sam. Jesus."

As officer Bill turned the key and Steve rubbed his wrists, he looked at Hipp and grinned blearily. He was clearly still drunk.

"Come on, you big prick," Hipp said, not unkindly. "Let's pour you into bed."

They started talking regularly after that night, mostly about the upcoming trial, which, when it finally happened, went well. Steve had been right. He could have done time. Should have, probably. It was his third DUI. But Hipp was a damn good lawyer and he kept him out of prison, though Steve lost his license, had to pay a hefty fine, and would be consulting regularly with a probation officer for the foreseeable future.

As they left the courthouse, Hipp was thinking that he'd seen just about enough of his former best friend. It was obvious that it was just a matter of time until Steve fucked up again, and the next time it happened not even Hippo would be able to keep his idiot ass from being locked up. And there was still the matter of that broken place in his brain. They walked together to the end of the concrete path that led from the courthouse to the road, and Hipp had every intention of turning left towards his car. But at the last minute he stopped. Steve was standing there stupidly, not knowing what to say.

"What are you doing tomorrow?" Hipp asked.

"Tomorrow. What are you...nothing. Why?"

"Want to go hunting?"

Steve face brightened visibly. For the first time since his colossal mistake had brought them back together, he broke into a full – no shit smile.

"Hell yeah!" he shouted. "I heard you got yourself a sweet Nosler."

Hipp nodded. "M48 Liberty," he said. "Laser scope."

"Jesus. Those go for over a grand."

"Almost two," Hipp said, leaving it at that. "What are you shooting these days?"

"I got the same Remington 783 I've had for years," Steve answered.

"It's a decent gun," Hipp said. "Though I doubt you can hit a damn thing with it." He smiled, and Steve smiled wider.

"We'll see. Guess you'll have to pick me up. You know, no license and all."

"Yeah. I know. I'll be at your place at four a.m. Don't forget to set an alarm or I'll kick the crap out of your front door and wake up all your neighbors."

"Jesus, don't do that. Everybody hates me already. I'll be awake, wearing my stylish orange."

"See that you are."

They shook hands, their first physical contact since their reunion.

"Thanks for keeping me out of stir," Steve said.

Hippo just nodded, and walked to his car.

His alarm sounded at two-thirty. At first, when he looked at the obscenely early hour on the digital clock, he couldn't remember why it was going off. Then it came to him. "Hunting," he said aloud.

He got up, made a pot of coffee, which, minus one cup, he poured into a thermos. While he was downing the wake-up joe, he pulled the Nosler out of its case and made sure it was good and clean. He glanced at his watch. He didn't have to leave to get Steve for another hour. It was too much time.

Hipp had wanted to be sure to get up early to get everything ready for the outing, but he hadn't counted on the amount of time it would allow for thinking.

It wasn't all bad, seeing Steve again. Although their meetings since that first late-night phone call had focused more on Steve's DUI than anything else, they had shared a good memory or two. It was Steve that had mentioned the woodpecker. Perhaps that had been part of the reason Hipp had suggested they go hunting.

If they were going to start hanging out again for real, Hipp reasoned, hunting would be a good start. Their best times were the times spent in the woods, even when they didn't get a deer, which had happened more often than they cared to admit.

But the woods also poked at the broken place in his brain with a sharp, angry stick.

Hipp opened that back hatch of his car, a black Lincoln Navigator. It was a far cry from the Datsun. He hadn't thought about that car in a long time, but this early morning it found its way into his awareness, tied forever with that dark night. He shook his head as he climbed behind the wheel, hit the buttons that heated the front seats. *Enough,* he told himself. *Either you're doing this or not. But enough!*

Steve, apparently worried that Hipp might keep his word

about pounding on the door, was sitting on the cement stoop in front of his place. He lived in the same house he'd lived in when they were kids. It was his now, as both of his parents had passed. Steve was not the conscientious homeowner that his father had been; the place was rundown, a lot like Steve himself.

But he was smiling as Hipp put the Lincoln in park and pushed another button, lifting the hatch for Steve to toss his rifle in the back. As he got into the passenger seat he reached inside of his bright orange jacket and pulled out a six-pack. "Not stealing it from Dad anymore. The garage fridge is mine now."

Hipp nodded. "I wonder if it will taste as good. I think horking it from your old man was part of the magic."

"For sure. But still just the one six," Steve said.

'Of course. Remember the rule."

They both spoke at the same time, reciting the edict they'd decided upon when they were still teenagers. "Always stay slightly less drunk than the deer."

"Besides," said Hipp, "I don't need to trash my career getting a dee-wee of my own."

"I would totally represent you in court," Steve said.

"I would totally go to jail."

It wasn't a long drive to the access road, but the snow was coming down steadily and Steve had already cracked open his first beer, more than enough of a violation to get them into deep shit should they get pulled over for travelling at an imprudent speed. So Hipp took it slow and they rode without saying much.

"Got any tunes in this bucket?" Steve asked.

Hipp turned to look at him, giving him an "are you shitting me?" look. He reached to his cup holder and grabbed a small remote. Pushing "play" dramatically, the car was filled with the bludgeoning guitar of Tony Iommi playing "War Pigs."

"Sabbath is kind of passé now, Hipp. Got any NWA?"

"Fuck you. That's not music. Besides, they're old news now too."

"You sound just like *your* old man now. He used to say the same thing about your metal."

Hipp laughed, conceding the point. "For him it was Benny Goodman or nothing," he said.

They were driving down the unpaved access road now, the Lincoln's transaxle automatically slipping into four-wheel drive. This impressive feature didn't escape Steve's attention.

"If this car was a chick I'd probably drop my load in my shorts as soon as it looked at me."

"It's pretty sweet." Hipp left it at that. He had no desire to rub anything in Steve's face.

The end of the road was marked by a barrier that ran across the width of it. Hipp jockeyed the SUV around so that it would already be pointing in the right direction when the time came to leave. They took their rifles out of their cases. Hipp fastened the laser sight into place. Steve had an optical scope, far less impressive but more than adequate. They loaded in two shells each, another long-standing tradition. Unlike DeNiro and Walken they didn't buy into that "one-shot" shit. If you missed with your first, you could damn well fire off a second. And more than one deer had taken the first bullet and ran, wounded, needing another to seal the deal.

Hipp opened a beer as the tailgate slowly lowered itself. When it clicked, then finished shutting tight with a little electric motor whine, Steve said, "I'm telling you. Goo right in my shorts."

"You can stay here and fuck my car if you want to, pervert."

Steve handed Hipp two more beers, which he slipped into deep pockets on each side of his thermal pants. He put the other two into his own pockets. "Nah, that's okay," Steve said. "It's only our first date."

They began trekking into the woods. The snow was pretty deep once they left the road, which had been relatively clear, as a few of the hunters with plows usually made a push down the length of it every couple of days. The further into the trees they went the higher they had to lift their legs to make their way. By the time they reached the Maple Tree they were winded. Hipp pointed to the trunk. "Wanna sit for a few?"

"Jesus Christ, yes! I feel like I'm gonna hurl and I'm not even drunk."

They tramped the snow down so that they didn't sink in up to their necks when they squatted. Each pulled a second brew from their pockets and gave the caps a twist. Without looking at each other they clinked the bottles together. "Skoal," they said in unison.

A long period of quiet ensued, punctuated a while later when the final two beers were opened, tapped together and cheered.

"You know, the sun won't be up for a while yet," Steve said at last. "We should probably plan the hunt."

"Do you want me to drive?" Hippo asked.

"Don't be a twat. You know you're the better shot."

They stood and surveyed the area. Hipp pointed to the left. "It's grown pretty dense over there. Might be promising. Can you make your way in there without tipping off every deer in the forest?"

"I will...after this!" Steve reached inside his jacket and pulled out a joint.

"Aw, man! Are you serious?" His tone was chastising, but his face showed desire.

"Lighten up, James," Steve said as he lit the doob. After a serious hit, he held it out to Hippo.

"Shit," Hippo said, reaching for the joint.

By the time they finished it several minutes later they were sitting again. "I'll be far stealthier now," Steve said.

"You'll shoot your eye out, kid," Hippo quoted.

Steve laughed for a long time before managing to say, "I fucking love that movie."

"Me too. Every time he starts talking about the Red Ryder I think about…"

"The woodpecker!" Steve finished. "Poor little fucker never knew what hit him."

Without really thinking, Hippo said, "I know how he felt."

Steve's face seemed to freeze in place. He stared straight ahead, suddenly unable to look at Hipp.

"Look man," he said finally, "I guess we gotta talk about it sooner or later."

"No, we don't," said Hippo.

"I felt like a shit as soon as they started talking about it. I felt like a shit because even though I was fucking burned as hell at you, I didn't want to see you go through that."

Since Steve didn't take the out, Hippo figured he might as well respond. "You felt like a shit because you knew you were going to let them do it."

"Yeah. I did. As soon as they talked Missy into it, I knew."

"I always thought me and Missy were cool," Hippo said. "I thought she liked me."

"Missy liked Missy," Steve said. "I didn't really figure that out till after I married her, but it's true now and it was true then."

"Even so," said Hipp, "you just *sat there!*" His voice was louder than he intended.

"Shh, dude. The deer."

"Yeah, the deer," Hippo said, growing quiet again. "I saw you smile," he said, almost under his breath.

"You had piss in your eyes. You couldn't see anything."

"Fuck you."

The silence between them was heavy now. "I never thought you'd come back from that," Steve said finally. "By Monday, ever kid at Woodland knew about it. Even the freshmen were laughing at you."

"I remember," said Hippo, his voice hollow now.

"But you did. You came back. Maybe not that year, but Christ, Hipp! Look at you. You're driving a fucking Lincoln, man. And me? I'm not even allowed to drive at all. I was supposed to have it all and you were supposed to be permanently scarred."

"What makes you think I wasn't?"

"Well, one of us is a hopeless, divorced alchy, and one of us is a distinguished lawyer."

"Distinguished? I keep hopeless alchies out of prison and do an occasional real estate closing. That's hardly distinguished, Steve."

Steve was insistent. "One of us crapped out of college one week into his frosh year and one of us went to Harvard, for fuck's sake."

"Whatever."

After another long silence, Steve looked east. "Sunrise," he said.

"Alright, mister stealthy. Scout that rise. I'll post up in the Maple," Hippo said, pointing to the thicket he'd identified as promising earlier.

"Don't fall out of the tree. You're still too goddamn big for one guy to carry you out. It took five…" He stopped mid-sentence.

"Look, it's true whether you say it out loud or not," Hipp said brusquely.

"Yeah. Let's pretend I never brought it up."

"Ok. We can pretend," Hippo grunted.

Steve headed off.

Hippo watched him until he disappeared into the brush. Once Steve was out of sight, Hipp took a deep breath and let it out slowly. *Goddamn him!* he thought. Strapping his gun over his shoulder, he began to climb the tree. He knew that he'd need to be at least fifteen feet up to get a good shot off. He wasn't used to smoking pot; he hadn't since Cornell. But he made the climb without incident and found a branch sturdy enough to keep him aloft.

He pulled the rifle off his shoulder and pointed it at the ground to make sure the laser was go. The red dot dutifully appeared.

Steve was a good driver, even if he was a shit shot. It would take some time, but if there was a deer anywhere near them, Steve would push it toward Hippo.

But Hippo wasn't thinking about deer.

He was thinking about the broken place. He was fully cognizant of its existence. He even called it that by that name: The Broken Place, with capital letters to make it a living thing. He pictured it as an actual blackened, cracked spot on his brain. Somewhere on the occipital lobe, he imagined. Even during the string of triumphs that had come after high school, he thought about it every day, closed his eyes and actually saw it. It was there in the morning when he woke up, often after a turbulent night of far too-vivid dreams. It followed him through the day like a stalker, and it was waiting for him when he collapsed into bed at night.

Now, as he felt the cold wind push the snow sideways across his line of sight, he felt The Broken Place growing. He'd only smoked a little, and three beers didn't do the damage to him at forty-nine that it had at seventeen, but he wasn't feeling right. Not right at all.

Why the hell did he have to bring it up? I was willing to say nothing! Does it still make him smile to think of his fucking girlfriend drizzling all over my fucking face? His wife? His fucking ex-wife bartender slut whore...

He felt nauseous. His breathing was fast, shallow. He put his hand inside his orange jacket and touched his chest. His heart was pounding. That would never do. He'd have to get his shit together fast. If Steve drove a deer to him now he'd miss it by an entire area code.

But still his thoughts raced. *I should have left him in that fucking jail cell. Maybe then he'd feel a tiny speck of what I felt...what I **feel**.*

With every ounce of discipline he could muster, Hipp began to slow his ragged breathing. Under his cold fingers he felt his heartrate begin to ramp down. He regained control of his body, but his brain was having none of it. Something was very wrong.

Off to the left Hipp heard a rustling. Instinctively he raised the rifle. There was enough light now that he could see the thick growth moving. He aimed carefully and waited. A moment later, about ten yards behind the movement he caught sight of Steve's orange vest, so he knew it was definitely an animal that was shaking the scrub.

Steve knew he'd gotten the buck into the right position. From where he stood he could make out Hipp's form in the tree through the blowing snow. The deer was ten yards ahead of him. He'd moved it slowly and carefully. The buck wasn't really even aware he was being driven, he just felt compelled to move in this direction. Now Steve saw it clearly for the first time since he'd started pushing him. He was an eight pointer, huge – proud.

"Take the shot, Hipp," he whispered. "Take the fucking shot."

A second later he caught sight of something moving near him. He looked down and saw a red dot on his chest.

From the highway, just at the entrance to the dirt road that led into the woods, a couple of kids with BB guns heard a rifle report.

"We better not go in," the smaller boy said to his bigger friend. "Sounds like hunters."

ABOUT THE AUTHOR

S.J. Varengo is a married father of two adult children. He lives in Upstate New York despite dire warnings. His published works include a volume of short fiction (*Welcome Home*), the Cerah of Quadar fantasy series, the Cleanup Crew thriller series, and the SpyCo novella series, which he co-writes with series creator Craig A. Hart. These two gibrones also co-host the best literary podcast in the world, possibly the galaxy, *Good Sentences*.

facebook.com/sjvarengo
twitter.com/PapaV
bookbub.com/authors/s-j-varengo

Made in United States
North Haven, CT
14 October 2022

25436665R00091